Dani's heart jolted in her chest.

Of course he would be standing with the sun at his back, putting her at even more of a disadvantage—as if she wasn't utterly disadvantaged anyway, in faded jeans and a T-shirt, and with her hair scraped back in a plait.

Rising to her feet, Dani studied her neighbor and her ex-ex-ex-boyfriend who evidently had finally decided to return after another extended absence.

"Well, if it isn't Mr. Commitment himself. Looking good, Carter."

It was a sad fact that he was drop-dead gorgeous: tall and muscled, with sun-bleached hair and killer blue eyes. Whatever he had been up to since he'd last climbed out of her bed and walked out the door hadn't detracted any from his appeal.

But she had been burned by Carter Rawlings a total of three times, and as far as she was concerned, that was two times too many.

Dear Reader,

High-Stakes Bride was always going to be a ranch story, because Carter Rawlings—the sixth and final member of my Down Under SAS team—has a strong link with the land. When I planned the book, the solution to who would finally tame my most elusive bachelor yet was simple— Dani Marlow, the girl next door. What I didn't understand until I began writing was how deep the secret of Dani's past went and just how wide-ranging the repercussions would prove to be. Dani turned out to be a headstrong, complex heroine, a fitting match for Carter, a seasoned assault specialist who is faced with the biggest challenge of his life: keeping Dani safe.

Enjoy!

Fiona Brand

FIONA BRAND
HIGH-STAKES
Bride

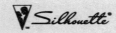

INTIMATE MOMENTS™

Published by Silhouette Books

America's Publisher of Contemporary Romance

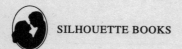 SILHOUETTE BOOKS

ISBN 0-373-27473-4

HIGH-STAKES BRIDE

Copyright © 2006 by Fiona Walker

This edition published by arrangement with Harlequin Books S.A.

® and TM are trademarks of Harlequin Books S.A., used under license. Trademarks indicated with ® are registered in the United States Patent and Trademark Office, the Canadian Trade Marks Office and in other countries.

Visit Silhouette Books at www.eHarlequin.com

Printed in U.S.A.

Books by Fiona Brand

Silhouette Intimate Moments

Cullen's Bride #914
Heart of Midnight #977
Blade's Lady #1023
Marrying McCabe #1099
Gabriel West: Still the One #1219
High-Stakes Bride #1403

Silhouette Books

Sheiks of Summer
"Kismet"

FIONA BRAND

has always wanted to write. After working eight years for
the New Zealand Forest Service as a clerk, she decided
she could spend at least that much time trying to get a
romance novel published. Luckily, it only took five years,
not eight. Fiona lives in a subtropical fishing and diving
paradise called the Bay of Islands with her two children.

Prologue

Twenty-two years ago, Dawson, New Zealand

Eight-year-old Dani Marlow's eyes flicked open in the dark. Icy moonlight filtered through the thin drapes pulled across her window, turning the pink quilt on her bed a frosted grey and bleaching the floorboards silver.

The sound that had woken her came again. Not the skeletal scrape of the clump of small trees that grew outside her window, or the ancient creaking of the oak that shaded most of the front lawn, but the sharp clink of metal against metal.

Breath suspended in her throat, she lay rigid, eyes fixed on the cracked plaster of the ceiling as she strained to listen. Time passed. The wind strengthened, the cold palpable as it rattled branches and whispered through desiccated leaves. Slowly, the tension ebbed from her limbs, her lids drooped and she began the warm drift back into sleep.

Glass shattered, the sound as explosive as a gunshot, jackknifing her out of bed. Bare feet hit the icy cold of the floor and, for a terrifying moment, Dani lost the sense of where she was—and *when*.

Light flooded through the gap where her bedroom door stood ajar, momentarily blinding her. Blankly, she registered footsteps, the crash of overturned furniture. A dull thud followed by an anguished cry shocked her out of her immobility.

Heart pounding, she wrenched her wardrobe door wide and fumbled through layers of clothing, fighting the frantic urge to burrow into the musty storage space and hide. She hadn't been dreaming, what was happening was real. *He* was here—*now*. Somehow he had found them again, and this time he had gotten inside the house. She didn't understand why or how it happened, just that no matter where they moved to, sooner or later, it did.

For a frantic moment she couldn't find what she was looking for, then her fingers closed on the stick she kept there. The wood was smooth where she'd peeled the bark away, and as heavy as a baseball bat. She had made it three months ago at the last place they had lived, when a neighbour had seen a man watching their flat and reported him to the police. They had managed to get away when the police cruiser had arrived and frightened him off. The time before they hadn't been so lucky. Susan had ended up in hospital with cracked ribs and a concussion, and Dani had gone into care.

Stomach tight, Dani edged along the narrow hall and halted in the doorway to the kitchen. A silver shape arrowed through the air. She ducked as the kettle hit the wall, spraying water. Simultaneously a loud bang was followed by a burst of blue light as the electrical mains above her head blew, plunging the house into darkness. Soaked and shivering, blinking to clear the flash of the explosion and adjust to the much dimmer moonlight pouring through the kitchen window, Dani struggled to make sense of the black shadow grappling with her mother.

Susan Marlow, clearly visible in a long pale nightgown, struck out, knocking the shadow back and abruptly the scene made sense. The shadow was a man dressed all in black, his hands, his face—every part of him blanked out—except for a narrow strip where his eyes glittered.

He swung, his arm a blur. Susan crumpled and, with a fierce cry, Dani launched herself. The stick arced down, crashing into the only part of him she could see, his eyes. The jarring force of the blow numbed her fingers and sent the stick spinning. A split second later she was flung through the air, for a timeless moment tumbling....

When Dani came to she lay sprawled at an angle, half under the kitchen table. Pain throbbed at the back of her head as she dragged herself into a sitting position and clung to a table leg for support.

He was at the sink. He had taken off what she now realized was a balaclava and was washing his face. As he turned, the glow from a flashlight uplit a broad chest and powerful shoulders, dark hair cut close against his skull, and a face that was nightmarishly distorted. Blood streamed from a swollen, misshapen nose and a livid cut below one eye where the flesh had peeled open revealing the glistening white of bone—the effect like something out of a horror movie.

Clutching his face to stem the flow of blood, he stumbled into the tiny lounge, the flashlight beam flickering over broken furniture and shards of glass as he stepped through the window he'd smashed to get into the house and merged with the night.

Dani huddled by the kitchen table, spine jammed against the wall. Freezing cold filtered through her pajamas, spreading like liquid ice as she stared through the wreckage of their home, gaze fastened on the empty rectangle of pure black where the window frame was pushed up.

Long seconds ticked by, and slowly, minute-by-minute, the extent of her victory settled in, steadying her. For the first time she'd had the courage to hit out, and she had hurt him—enough that he'd had to leave. When she was certain he wasn't coming back, she crawled over to Susan and her heart almost stopped. Susan was white and still, and for a terrifying moment she was certain she was dead.

Frantically, she clutched at her shoulder and shook. Susan's head lolled, her eyes flickered and relief shuddered through Dani.

Forcing herself to her feet, she limped to the kitchen counter, reached high and grabbed the first aid box. Setting the container beside Susan, she pried off the lid, found the cotton wool and disinfectant and began dabbing at the split on Susan's lip and the grazes on her jaw and temple. Susan flinched, but didn't wake up.

Panic gripped Dani as she fetched a bag of frozen peas from the freezer, wrapped them in a tea towel and set the makeshift icepack against the side of Susan's face. She should call an ambulance, but Susan had said not to call *anyone* because if the welfare people got to hear what was happening, they'd take her away—this time maybe for good. The same went for the police. As badly as they needed help, they didn't need what came with it. According to Susan the paper trail left them too exposed, and *he* was clever. It was one of the ways he used to find them.

Stoically, Dani continued cleaning away the blood then set about making up a bed up on the floor. She didn't know how long it would be before Susan woke up, but, in the freezing cold of a South Island winter, she had to be kept warm. Shivering, her stomach tight with fear, Dani lay under the pile of quilts with Susan, waiting for her to wake up.

Blankly, she stared at the open window.

The glass was gone, so closing it was a waste of

time, but she should have pulled the curtains to help stop the cold air pouring into the house. It wasn't snowing or sleeting, but there would be a frost; ice already glittered on the sill. Shuddering, she wrenched her gaze free. She hadn't wanted to go near the window because somehow the magnetic black space was part of *him*.

With an effort of will, she forced herself to concentrate on Susan. Her breathing sounded better, although it still had a catch as if even sleeping, she was hurting.

Dani moved closer, shielding Susan from the window and the freezing stream of cold air, misery condensing into a piercing ache.

They would be all right. They just had to move again.

And this time they *would* disappear.

Chapter 1

Four years later, Jackson's Ridge, New Zealand

The noonday sun burned into the darkly tanned skin of twelve-year-old Carter Rawlings's shoulders as he slid down the steep scrub-covered hill just below his parents' house. Grabbing the gnarled branch of a pohutukawa tree, he swung and launched off a platform of black rock that jutted out from the bank, the tip of one of the ancient lava flows that had made its mark on Jackson's Bay and a string of other beaches stretching along the east coast of the North Island.

Wincing at the heat pouring off the sand, he loped down the beach to check out the new kid who had just moved next door.

A pair of gulls wheeled above, shrieked and swooped low, beady eyes hopeful. Carter slowed to a walk as his feet sank into the cool damp sand that delineated the high-tide mark. Keeping his gaze fixed on the thin body of the boy, he searched the pockets of his shorts. "Sorry guys, no food today."

Normally he remembered to grab a slice of bread for the gulls, but today it had been all he was capable of to sit at the table once his chores were done and bolt down a sandwich before being excused. The new kid was the first exciting thing that had happened all summer. Maybe it shouldn't have been, but in Jackson's Ridge, a tiny coastal settlement that had flat-lined long before he was born, a new neighbour ranked right up there with the apocalypse.

The surf-casting rod the boy was holding flicked back, then forward. Silvery nylon filament shot out across the waves. Bait and sinker hit the surface of the water just beyond the break line and sank.

Great cast. Perfect. The kid had done it like a pro, except, Carter now realized, the boy, Dani, who had moved in the previous evening, wasn't a "he."

She had red hair scraped into a long plait over one shoulder and a blue T-shirt plastered against her skinny torso. Her faded cut-offs were soaked and she'd lost one of her sneakers in the tide. He caught the glint of a tiny gold stud in one lobe. A tomboy, maybe, but definitely not a boy.

He shoved his hands in the pockets of his shorts. "Hi."

For an answer she stepped into the water foaming just inches from her feet and waded in until the water eddied around her knees. Her rod dipped as she wound in slack line; a few seconds later it shivered as something nibbled at the bait. She moved forward another step, playing the fish.

Automatically, Carter studied the swell. The waves came in in sets. Jackson's Bay was sheltered so it wasn't usually a problem, but every now and then a big one arrived. "Careful. There's a rip just there, sometimes it—"

Water surged, she staggered. A second wave followed, forming a sloppy breaker, and with a yelp she went down, the rod flipping into the surf.

Carter lunged, turning side-on to the wave as his fingers latched onto her arm. The water went slack then almost instantly surged back out to sea, the pull dragging the sand from beneath his feet.

"*Let go.*" Staggering upright she wrenched free, dashed water from her eyes then dove into the next wave and came up with the rod.

Cool. Carter wiped salt water from his face as he watched her wind in the line. She hadn't needed his help. "I guess your name's Danielle."

Her dark gaze was dismissive as she strode, dripping, from the water.

Carter didn't let it get to him. He had never met a girl yet who could resist him, let alone one who hardly knew he existed. He was used to girls noticing him: he had killer blue eyes.

Shrugging, he trailed after her as she followed a line of scuffed footprints to a battered tackle box and a beach towel. With cursory movements she examined the chewed bait dangling from the hook and flipped the lock on the reel. His gaze fixed on the set of her jaw and the fine sprinkling of freckles across her nose.

Time for phase two. "*Is* Danielle your name?"

A lean tanned hand slapped the lid of the tackle box closed. "Get lost."

Bemused, Carter watched as she snatched up the tackle box and towel, strode across the sand and took the rocky path up to the Galbraith house.

She was tall for a girl—although nowhere near as tall as he was—with a lean lanky build and a face that would have been a knockout if she hadn't been scowling. According to his mother she was the same age as he was, which meant she'd be in his class at school.

Not Danielle, Dani.

He shrugged. The conversation hadn't exactly been riveting, but…

He grinned as he strolled back home.

She liked him. He could tell.

"He's a pain." Dani ignored her mother's frown as she propped her ancient fishing rod against the side of the house, removed the ragged shred of bait and tossed it to a hungry gull.

Jaw set, she stared at the distant view of the horizon, and the hazy line where sea met sky, her heart still pounding from the embarrassing near-death experience followed by the hike up the hill.

She had been *that* close to landing the fish. If what's-his-name Rawlings hadn't come along she would have caught it—guaranteed.

Susan sent her a warning glance. "His name's Carter and he's your next-door neighbour."

For how long? "That doesn't mean I have to like him."

Dani wrung out her still-dripping plait, toed off her remaining sneaker and strode to her new room to change. When she was dressed, she grimaced at the pile of wet things in the laundry basket. She had lost a sneaker. Her mother had been too preoccupied to notice that detail, but when she did, she would go crazy. Susan had been out of work for the past three months, ever since her last job as a counter assistant at one of the town-and-country stores in Mason had dissolved after the business had merged with a larger firm. In theory they couldn't afford to eat—let alone spend money on shoes.

Dani stared at the unfamiliar bedroom; the pretty bed with its white-and-green patterned quilt, the elegant lines of the dressers and the needlework sampler on the wall. Not for the first time the strangeness of moving into someone else's home, of being surrounded with someone else's things, hit her. She'd been used to bare rooms and minimal furniture—all of it impersonal and second-hand—of keeping clothing and possessions sparse and relationships nonexistent, so that if they had to pick up and leave in a hurry they wouldn't lose too much. For four years the isolation of that existence had worked—until they'd landed in Mason and Susan had met Galbraith.

After years of staying on the move and never putting down roots there was no way she could like the permanence that was building here—no matter how much either of them craved it. This life—the settled-in comfort and the homeliness—just didn't fit with the tactics that had kept them safe.

Dani trailed, barefooted, back to the kitchen, eyeing a line-up of gloomy oil paintings in the hallway and taking care not to touch any of the highly polished furniture or the pretty ornaments placed on dainty occasional tables.

Everything about the Galbraith house radiated family and permanence—from the slightly battered antiques to the family photos depicting grandparents, aunts, uncles and cousins: generation upon generation of Galbraiths—so many of them that every time she looked around she felt exactly as she had when she'd lost her footing and been swept into the surf—off balance and floundering.

Eyeing the crystal chandelier that hung from the ornately molded ceiling in the dining room, she stepped into the kitchen. Her mother was placing a large bowl filled with apples in the centre of the table—one of the many little touches Susan Marlow did to make a room look just so, whether they were living in a crummy little one-bedroom flat or a caravan.

Dani glanced around the high airy room with its antique dressers and air of fading elegance. Or on an impressive homestead sited on a large sheep and cattle station.

She could see why her mother had been bowled over by Robert Galbraith and the Rawlings family next door—and why she liked it here. Who wouldn't? As people went, they had it all: nice homes, acres of land, and their own private beach that was so mesmerizingly beautiful she had just wanted to stand there and stare.

Her mother finished setting the lunch table and stood back to admire the gleam of porcelain and old silver. She lifted a brow. "Carter's a nice-looking boy. I think you do like him."

Fierceness welled up in Dani. "I don't."

Boyfriends weren't on her agenda—they couldn't be. She'd seen the way girls at school mooned after them, and the way Susan had changed. If she were going to depend on anyone, it would be herself. From what she'd seen, falling in love was nothing but trouble.

The bark of dogs and the sound of footsteps on the veranda heralded Robert Galbraith's arrival. Seconds later, he appeared in the kitchen doorway, tall and broad-shouldered, with a kind of blunt, weathered handsomeness that seemed to go hand-in-hand with the rugged contours of Galbraith Station.

Warily, Dani watched as her mother's face lit up, and noted Galbraith's corresponding expression. Her mother was an attractive woman, not beautiful exactly, but tall and striking, and today she looked a lot younger than thirty-five. She might not have a mil-

lion dollars, but with her hair piled on top of her head
and the simple but elegant clothes she was wearing,
she looked it.

Galbraith set his hat on a small dresser just inside
the door. Dani's head snapped around, almost giving her whiplash as she instinctively avoided wit-
nessing the kiss. A count to ten later, she risked a
look.

Ten seconds hadn't been long enough.

The meal stretched on interminably. Dani ate
bites of her sandwich, helped down by sips of water
while she observed Robert Galbraith, reluctantly
fascinated. He was a new phenomenon in her life—
the only man she had ever known Susan to date—
and now they were living with him.

Abruptly, a nightmare image of the shadowy man
cleaning up at the sink after he'd broken into their
cottage made her stomach clench. She hadn't told
Susan she had seen his face, or that she had injured
him. They had simply packed and run, leaving everything but the necessities behind and driving
through the night.

Dani transferred her attention to Susan, her gaze
fiercely protective. There was no question; they
would have to leave, and the sooner the better. The
risk Susan was taking was unacceptable. In every attack she had always been the focus. The only time
Dani had been hurt had been when she had finally
gotten up the courage to run at him and he had swat-
ted her away like a fly.

When Galbraith finally left the lunch table, Dani

began clearing dishes. As she piled plates and cutlery in the sink, the words erupted out of her. "We're making a big mistake."

Susan's expression turned sharp. "For the first time in years I'm making the right choice. He's asked me to marry him."

Dani froze in the act of turning a tap. "Does he know?"

"*No*." Susan scraped leftover food scraps into the compost bucket under the sink. "And don't look like that, missy."

Dani clamped her jaw and retrieved the empty salad bowl from the table. She stared at the fragile porcelain. It was so fine and translucent she could see the shadow of her fingers through it. "We're not safe here."

That was an understatement. They were sitting ducks. After years of lying low, of Susan working for cash under the table—even forgoing welfare payments because that would pinpoint where they were—of never forming relationships, let alone dating, the abrupt turnaround was stunning. A marriage meant legal paperwork and bank accounts. The paper trail would point a huge neon arrow in their direction.

Susan snatched the bowl and rinsed it. "Yes. We *are*." The bowl hit the draining board with a clatter. Susan's fingers gripped the edge of the bench, her face abruptly white.

Dani stared at her mother, heart pounding. Susan was tall and lean and strong. She'd worked all sorts of jobs from legal secretary to shop assistant to picking fruit. They might be poor, but she had always prided herself on having the constitution of an ox. Apart from the occasional sniffle, neither of them was ever sick. "What's wrong?"

Susan straightened. "I'm pregnant."

Dani stared at her mother. Of all the answers she might have expected, that hadn't ever been one of them. Suddenly the move and the way her mother was behaving began to make sense. "Does Galbraith know?"

"His name's Robert. And no, not yet. I've only just realized myself."

The expression on her mother's face made Dani feel even sicker. Dani's father had left before she'd been born, the only remnant of that brief relationship a name on her birth certificate. The concept that Galbraith would willingly take on not only a wife but *two* children—one of them not his own—was staggering.

Her mother retrieved the salad bowl, examined it for cracks and rinsed it. "Don't worry, we'll manage—one way or another."

"What if *he* finds out?"

Susan's jaw tightened. "I don't want to hear you mention him again—*it's finished*. He hasn't found us for four years. He won't find us now."

The snort of a horse drew Dani's attention. She stared at the scene unfolding in the paddock immediately adjacent to the house.

Carter was outside with Galbraith and two tall bay

horses. She watched as Carter swung smoothly into the saddle. Dust plumed from restless hooves as the animals paced out of an open stock gate, hard-packed muscle rippling beneath satiny skin. Two dogs trotted alongside, tongues lolling. Dani blinked, spellbound. The scene was idyllic—like everything on Galbraith—and, like the endless rhythm of the sea dragging the sand from beneath her feet, it was steadily undermining her resolve. She was used to cutting ties, the idea of holding on made her dizzy.

Dazed, Dani realized that, like Susan, she didn't want to leave. She wanted to stay so badly it hurt.

Susan tugged at her plait. "You just wait, you'll change your mind about boys one day."

For a heartthrob like Carter Rawlings? She'd rather live in a soap opera.

She might be young, but ever since she was six years old and *he* had broken into their house for the first time, she had known that men spelled more trouble than she ever wanted to take.

In her limited experience, if you could lose them you were lucky.

Chapter 2

Present day, Jackson's Ridge, New Zealand

The sun was high, the air rippling with heat, the breeze hot and dry as it rustled through native manuka trees and flipped a strand of hair loose from Dani Marlow's plait. As she slid from the seat of her tractor, she noted the direction of the breeze—a southerly—not the drought-breaking northerly she and every other farmer on the East Coast needed. They'd had a dry year, followed by an even drier summer, and the disastrous weather had desiccated the soil, killed most of the grass and undermined Galbraith Station's already shaky financial position.

Properties all up and down the coast were selling

at rock-bottom prices, and the sharks were queuing—most notably a fancy out-of-town syndicate that, rumor had it, was determined to turn the small farming community of Jackson's Ridge into an upmarket golf course and beach resort.

The Barclays, who owned a block just up the coast, were contemplating selling after a fire burnt down their barn and decimated their maize crop. Another neighbour, old Mr. Stoddard, had rung just last night to let her know that instead of the extension on his mortgage he'd requested, the bank had sent him a letter advising him that his interest rate was going up. He was hanging on, but at seventy years of age, he had better things to do than watch his cows die of thirst and fight a bank that no longer had any confidence in his ability to service his loan.

Dust whirled, peppering Dani's eyes as she crouched down to check the underside of the tractor. It didn't take a diesel mechanic to diagnose what was wrong with the ancient Ferguson—affectionately labeled the Dinosaur. The oil sump was leaking.

Muttering beneath her breath, she straightened and walked to the small trailer coupled to the rear of the tractor and extracted a new bolt with its accompanying nut and washer from the "breakdown" toolbox. Shoving the wisp of hair behind her ear, she grabbed a wrench, a socket and a rag streaked with oil from the last breakdown, crawled beneath the Dinosaur and turned on her back.

For the third time in a month the same bolt had worked loose, jolted out by the bone-shaking ruts and potholes of Galbraith Station's fast-disintegrating stock roads. Each time she'd gone into town and bought a slightly larger bolt, the metal of the sump, warped with constant flexing and worn thin by extreme age, had disintegrated enough that the bolt had shaken loose. The sump itself was about to expire, but because the tractor was so old, obtaining another part would be close to impossible. She had two options: get an engineer to manufacture a part, which would cost a small fortune, or buy a new tractor, which would cost more money than she could raise this year—or the next.

Oil slid down the backs of her hands and her wrists as she pushed the sump back into place and lined up the bolt holes. With a deft movement, she slipped the bolt through and held it in place as she awkwardly reached around the solid-steel chassis to slide the washer and the nut onto the shaft of the bolt, straining until the thread caught and the nut wound smoothly on.

Clamping the wrench around the nut to hold it still, she began the delicate process of tightening the bolt, a quarter turn at a time with the socket in the confined space, careful not to stress the tired metal by screwing the bolt in too tightly. Long seconds later, arms aching, she loosened off the wrench and the socket, set the tools down in the dust and simply lay in the shadows beneath the tractor, the tautness of her muscles turning to liquid as she let herself go boneless.

She was hot, sweaty and tired, and every part of

her ached. The summer had been the driest on record, and she'd been up since before dawn moving stock and checking water troughs. When she'd finished her morning round, she'd showered, changed and opened her physiotherapy practice, which occupied the old shearers' quarters. Her last appointment had been at three, after which she'd started loading hay onto the trailer and feeding out.

Even moving the cattle every day, rotating them from field to field, and grazing what was known as the "long acre"—the roadside grass—didn't allow her paddocks time to recover. Without rain, the grass couldn't grow, and there simply wasn't enough feed. She was already using her winter supply; when that was gone she would have to either start buying in feed she couldn't afford, or sell the entire herd, including the breeding cows.

She'd done the figures for selling early, and they weren't good. The cattle would be underweight, and the market would be low. The worst-case scenario was that she wouldn't make enough to cover the balloon payment that was due on the mortgage. If that happened, her half-brother, David, would lose the farm and his home.

The drought had already done its damage, and every day it continued the damage increased. Now, regardless of when it rained, they had already sustained a loss; it was only the magnitude of the loss that was in question.

Letting out a breath, she let her lids drift closed. She wouldn't sleep, but she was tired enough that the iron-hard dirt felt as soft as a feather bed. Slowly, inner tension seeped away, and her breathing evened out.

A small sound disturbed the silence. Liquid trickled down her arm. Her lids flickered.

Oil.

The Dinosaur was still leaking, this time from somewhere else, which meant the sump and the bolt could be side issues.

"Oh yeah, you're going to die on me soon," she muttered sleepily. "Just not yet."

Give me a couple more weeks, then it won't matter.

"If this rust heap is terminal," a low male voice murmured, "it better not be in my driveway."

Dani's heart jolted in her chest. She hadn't heard a vehicle, but that wasn't surprising. The rising wind hitting the tall line of poplar trees along the roadside was loud enough to muffle most sounds and, despite her resolve, she *had* fallen asleep. If she'd been fully conscious there was no way her closest neighbour, Carter Rawlings, would have sneaked up on her.

Grabbing the tools, she crawled out from beneath the Dinosaur and blinked into the afternoon sun. Of course he *would* be standing with the sun at his back, putting her at even more of a disadvantage—as if she wasn't utterly disadvantaged anyway in faded jeans and a T-shirt, leather boots that were crusted with dirt, and her hair scraped back in a plait.

Rising to her feet, Dani studied her neighbour and ex-ex-ex-boyfriend who, evidently, had finally decided to return to Jackson's Ridge after yet another extended absence.

"Well, if it isn't Mr. Commitment, himself." And if he said, "Hi, honey, I'm home," she wouldn't be responsible for her actions. "Looking good, Carter."

It was a sad fact that he *was* drop-dead gorgeous: tall and muscled with sun-bleached hair, a solid, nicely moulded jaw and those killer blue eyes.

Deftly, she stepped around him and replaced her tools in their box. "Long time no see."

And wasn't that just typical? The Rawlings family had lived next door to the Galbraiths forever, but Carter had always been too restless to stay in Jackson's Ridge. Despite being neighbours for eighteen years, the time Dani had actually spent with Carter had been little. When Carter had turned thirteen he had gone away to boarding school. From boarding school, he had gone directly into the army, then the Special Air Service. From that point on he had become even more elusive, only returning home for brief stints to visit his parents when he had leave. And lately, over the past six years, depending on the state of their relationship, to visit her.

"I've been busy."

"Evidently." Almost a whole year busy. But for the first time since they'd started dating six years ago she'd had the luxury of not worrying about exactly *what* he was doing, and how dangerous it was. As far as Dani was concerned it had been a productive year.

"I rang."

Dani wiped her hands on the rag and tossed it in the back of the trailer. "I got your messages."

"You didn't reply."

She cocked her head to one side and took a second look. Whatever Carter had been up to since he'd last climbed out of her bed and walked out the door hadn't detracted any from his appeal. Despite her detachment, her stomach did a funny little flip-flop. Her jaw tightened. She had been burned by Carter Rawlings a total of three times. As far as she was concerned, that was two times too many. The fact that the masochistic streak that kept her making the same mistake over and over was still in existence didn't make her happy. She was thirty, supposedly intelligent and independent. As far as she was concerned she had been inoculated *three* times. Somewhere there had to be a rule about that, and she wasn't about to break it.

She snapped the toolbox closed and fastened the lid. "I didn't see any point. We broke up."

He muttered something short and sharp beneath his breath. "Why isn't Bill fixing the tractor?"

Dani wedged the oilcan between the toolbox and the side of the trailer so it wouldn't shift when she negotiated the rutted drive to the house. The last thing she needed was to lose a can of oil. As inexpensive as it was, replacing it would blow her budget for the week, and with the mortgage falling due in a fortnight she was literally counting every cent. In theory she couldn't afford to eat. "I had to let Bill go two months ago. There's a recession, or hadn't you noticed?"

Maybe not. By the shiny glint of his brand-new four-wheel drive, she deduced that drought, recession and bottomed-out stock prices or not, Carter was doing all right.

"I've noticed." He jerked his head toward the tractor. "Why didn't you give Geoff a call?"

Geoff was the diesel mechanic based in town. He serviced most of the farm equipment locally. "Geoff costs forty dollars an hour. Fifty-five on a call-out."

Carter walked around the Dinosaur. Distracted, Dani noted the stiffness of his movements.

"You're telling me you've been fixing the tractor yourself?"

And the farm bike and the truck. If she lost the farm, she could probably open up in competition with Geoff's Diesels and make some real money.

Dani made a production of looking around. "Can't see anyone else. Must have been me."

Carter's stare was cold and disorientingly direct. "You're not going to make this easy, are you?"

Never again. "What's the matter? You got issues with women fixing machines?"

He stared at the tractor, then glanced back at Dani. "Yes."

The word was bitten out, clipped and cold, as if he had every right to an opinion. An involuntary shiver worked its way down her spine. She'd been angry at Carter for months—no, cancel that—*years,* and in all that time, she'd never imagined that he could be angry with her.

"I heard about Ellen. I'm sorry."

She fastened the lid of the toolbox with fingers that were abruptly clumsy. The loss of her adoptive aunt, Ellen Galbraith, still cut deep. Ellen had helped her through one of the toughest times in her life, when Susan and Robert had both been killed in a car accident; it had broken her heart to let her go. "She had a heart condition."

One that had manifested almost overnight, but must have been brewing for years. Ellen had had a bad case of the flu and had simply never gotten well. Confused by the symptoms, but suspicious, their local GP had run a series of tests, but by the time Ellen had been diagnosed as suffering from heart failure, massive damage had been done. She'd had a bypass operation, which had briefly improved her condition, but four months after the initial diagnosis, she had caught another bout of flu and slipped away in her sleep just hours later.

Clamping her jaw against the ache at the back of her throat, Dani gripped the worn steering wheel, and swung up into the Dinosaur's seat. "I've got to go."

He stepped toward the tractor, as if he was going to detain her, the motion faintly awkward.

Dani stared, arrested by the uncharacteristic clumsiness. "What's wrong with your leg?"

His gaze jerked to hers, and there was nothing lazy, intimate or even remotely friendly in the contact. For a moment she had the uncomfortable sensation she was looking at a complete stranger. "A gunshot wound."

For a blank moment she didn't know what to say or how to react. Carter was in the Special Air Service. It was hard to miss that fact when his high-risk, high-adrenaline career had destroyed their relationship. But coming face-to-face with the reality of a gunshot wound was shocking.

She stared at his broad back as he limped to his truck, studying the way he moved, the kinks in his posture that told her Carter was fresh out of rehab and still healing. Ever since Carter had gone into the military she had worried about the danger—whether they were involved or not, Carter's well-being mattered. "When?"

"Four months ago."

Her stomach tightened. Another piece of the puzzle fell into place. Two months ago she'd heard, courtesy of Nola McKay—the owner of Nola's Café—that Carter hadn't just been away on an extended tour of duty, he had been missing in action. The news, delivered with a latte and the rider that he had been rescued, had shocked her, but still disconnected and numb with the grief of Ellen's death, it had taken her another week before she'd gotten up the energy to do a search on the Internet. Eventually she had found a report that a soldier was missing in action in Borneo. The wording had been brief and clinical and hadn't included any details. Like the high-security classification on Carter's career, the report closed more doors than it opened.

She wished the fact that Carter had been shot didn't affect her, but it did. The past year had been hard, and it had changed her. She knew she'd gotten quieter and more withdrawn, but, unlike Carter, she still couldn't lay claim to being either cold or detached.

Carter eased into the driver's seat and she remembered his opening line—the reason he had stopped and spoken to her at all: she was blocking his driveway.

Letting out a breath, she turned the key. The tractor motor turned over, coughed then caught, the rumble loud enough to preclude conversation.

Relief loosened off the tension in the pit of her stomach. Gunshot wound or not, Carter was on his own. If he wanted female company, there were plenty of women in town who would be only too pleased to soothe his hurts and massage his sore muscles; women who were younger, prettier and a whole lot more fun than she ever planned on being.

She released the clutch. "There is a rule," she just had to keep reminding herself. "Three strikes, and you're out."

Chapter 3

Carter watched the retreating dust cloud, eased his leg into a more comfortable position and slammed his door closed.

The message screen of his cell phone glowed. Two missed calls and a message. The missed calls were both from his mother. Ever since he'd gotten back into the country both of his parents, who had retired to a popular resort town further up the coast a couple of years ago, had kept in daily contact. The fact that he had been taken prisoner had shaken them. The gunshot wound came a close second, but not by much. Despite his assurances, they insisted on keeping in close touch.

The text message was from Gabriel West, a long-time friend, ex–SAS sniper and leader of the private team that had flown into Borneo to rescue him.

Carter read the message and pressed Delete. Lately West had been abnormally solicitous and curious about what he was up to—and with whom. Along with everything else that had gone wrong lately, Carter was beginning to feel like he was being watched over by an overlarge hen.

Turning the key in the ignition, he manoeuvred the truck off the verge and into the entrance of his drive, barely noticing the weed-infested borders, or the fact that one of the smaller farm sheds had lost its roof in the last big storm.

He had to wonder just what he'd let slip when he'd been semi-conscious in the hospital. West was more than curious. Now he wanted to visit.

It was a fact that he did feel different. He still hadn't figured out exactly *what* had changed except that for months he'd felt unsettled—in the psychologist's jargon, "disengaged." Even when he'd finally been declared fit enough to resume light duties—translate that as pushing paper in an office—he'd felt like a square peg trying to fit into a round hole. The psychologist had diagnosed post-traumatic shock syndrome—maybe even an early mid-life crisis.

Carter frowned as he slowed for a bend. He liked things cut-and-dried, the idea that he was suffering from something as woolly and amorphous as some kind of mental and emotional breakdown ticked him off.

It was a fact that the months spent in captivity hadn't been a picnic. From beginning to end, what had happened had been a prime example of bad timing and bad luck.

The assignment to escort an Indonesian government official to the small village of Tengai hadn't been high-risk, or even particularly interesting. Carter had simply been in the wrong place at the wrong time. Two rival rebel factions had chosen that particular village to clash. When the shooting started, Carter had kept to task and protected the official, but when they had finally made it out of the building, their transport and backup were gone.

If they'd stayed inside and kept out of sight, in all probability they would have been in the clear, but one of the village children had been cut up by a ricochet and Carter had started to treat him. Two of the rebels who were still holed up in the village had accosted Carter at gunpoint, ignored the government official and demanded Carter leave with them.

They didn't want to kidnap a bureaucrat. What they needed was a trained medic.

After stripping the official of his suit, his watch and all of his cash, the men had herded Carter into the jungle, his weaponry, communications equipment and medical kit confiscated along with his boots.

Apart from the restricted diet—crazily enough, stolen army rations—and the hours spent kicking his heels under armed guard, nothing horrific had happened. He had been too useful. He'd treated two of the rebels for gunshot wounds, delivered a baby and dealt with a minor outbreak of dysentery. When he'd finally managed to slip away at night, four months after capture, all he'd had were his clothes, a knife he'd managed to steal and the remnants of his medical kit.

Without a compass—and travelling beneath a canopy that blocked both the sun and stars, burying him in either a soupy half light or impenetrable darkness—he had ended up travelling in a circle and had practically walked back into the rebel camp. A sentry had spotted him and fired, but the fact that he'd been hit at all was a miracle, and the sentry himself didn't register the hit. The rebels as a force were canny and elusive, but they weren't trained soldiers. They relied on surprise and the threat of their weapons—not accuracy.

A brief search was conducted, then abandoned, and Carter was able to put some distance between himself and the camp. After that, things had gotten a little hazy. He'd injected himself with morphine, lain up for a day, strapped his leg with his shirt then started to walk. The next day he'd found a small settlement and managed to get some food and water. With the help of the village midwife he'd extracted the bullet then had spent the next three days on his back in a small tin shack fighting off a fever.

With his leg heavily bandaged and seeping, Carter had been escorted by one of the villagers to the next village further down the valley, on the verge of the Kalimantan Lowlands. It was there he'd gotten the news that a private team was looking for him—not the army rescue squad he'd expected.

Apparently, after political pressure exerted by the government official who had been left kicking his heels in Tengai, the peacekeeping unit had been forced to withdraw from Borneo. The irony that the official he had been commissioned to protect from the rebels had left him hanging out to dry wasn't lost on Carter. Lately, with his luck, crossing the road had become dangerous.

Carter brought the truck to a halt in front of the sprawling, one-storied house, perched on a bluff above the bay. The house, which he'd bought from his parents along with the farm, was old and comfortable, hemmed by verandas and large sweeping lawns. A cooling breeze rustled through a clump of oleanders, the scent of the jasmine that grew wild in the garden filled his nostrils and over all was the fresh tang of the ocean. From where he was sitting, he could see the water, a broad sweep of blue stretching to the horizon.

Grabbing his suitcase from the back seat of the truck, he limped toward the porch, slid the key in the lock and pushed the door wide. The late-afternoon sun sent his shadow sliding over the faded hall carpet. The house was silent and deserted.

Stepping inside, he set the suitcase down and limped through to the empty kitchen, checking that the hot water was on. The couple he employed to mow the lawns and clean the house had been in. His gaze swept the clean lines of the kitchen counter and snagged on the blinking light of the answering machine. With resignation, he picked up the receiver and hit the play button.

One hang-up, two messages from an old girl-friend, Mia, wanting to know how he was after his "accident," and a call from his C.O. wanting to set up an appointment for his next round of assessments.

Carter hit the delete button. Six weeks after being airlifted to a hospital in Darwin, Australia, he'd been put on a routine flight into Auckland and had reported to his C.O.

The debrief hadn't been pleasant. Naturally, he had failed his medical exam. His psychological report had been even worse. His commander had been impressed by the fact that he would be able to walk without the aid of a stick, eventually, but the prognosis for resuming active service was grim.

The slug had entered at the rear of his upper thigh, ploughing south through the complex interweaving of muscles and ligaments to lodge just above his knee. It hadn't broken his femur or nicked an artery, but it had damaged practically everything else. He had extensive soft-tissue damage to all the main muscles, which had meant fun and games for the surgeon who'd done the reconstructive surgery, and the patella ligament, which supported his knee, had been damaged.

He had been lucky. If the bullet had travelled another two inches it would have shattered his knee.

Several weeks later, after further surgery to release adhesions and nerves caught in scar tissue, he had been able to straighten his leg, and for the first time since he'd been shot he had been able to walk without the aid of a stick, albeit painfully. From then on, his progress had been rapid. He didn't just want to walk. If he couldn't run, he couldn't pass the service medical exam—which meant he was finished for active duty. The bullet had missed vital organs, but it now looked as though it had taken out his career.

He could still serve in the regiment as an instructor if he wanted, but the offer hadn't made Carter happy.

He had lost months of his life in captivity and almost as much again in and out of hospitals. Now he'd been given six weeks to improve his mobility and his attitude.

His jaw tightened as he walked out onto the veranda and stared down the winding shell path that led to the beach. He hadn't been through months of pain and frustration to keep losing: he liked the life he'd had before and he wanted it back—and that included Dani.

If she would let him in.

She'd always been ultra independent and elusive. He'd had her door slammed in his face more than once—and always with justification. It was a fact that Special Forces was hard on relationships; his job took him away for months at a time. With the length of this last absence, he couldn't blame her for wanting out, but that didn't mean he was going to give up. He would bring her around—eventually.

She loved him.

All he had to do was convince her of that fact.

Dani drove the Dinosaur into the implement shed, turned off the ignition and climbed out of the bony metal seat. The silence after the loud rumbling of the engine was momentarily deafening.

She stared out into the soft early-evening light.

Carter was back. Finally.

Letting out a breath, she lowered herself onto an upturned bucket, for the moment comfortable with the dimness and the quiet.

She'd known he'd had to come back some time—she had expected him sooner than this—but still, seeing him had knocked her sideways, and finding out he had been injured had been a shock. Ever since he'd joined the army she'd nursed the fear that he'd get hurt, and now it had happened.

She shifted position and the faint twinge of stiffness in her own leg registered, and other even more unwelcome memories flooded back.

Six years ago she had been involved in a car accident that had killed both her mother and Robert Galbraith, and injured her. She had been home from Mason, taking a break from her first full year in physiotherapy practice. She had volunteered to drive Susan and Robert into town and drop them at the golf club for their weekly golf date before continuing on to pick up David, who had spent the night at a friend's place. Out of sheer practicality they had taken Robert's car, since he had had a trunk large enough to hold both sets of golf clubs. She could remember trying to avoid a large truck, the wheels of the car sliding in the layer of gravel on the verge. The car had fishtailed and the truck had slammed into the side of the vehicle. They'd rolled, ending upside-down in the ditch.

Dani had broken a leg and received cuts on her face and arms from the shattered windshield. Her mother, who was seated in the rear, had received the brunt of the impact from the truck and had died instantly. Robert Galbraith hadn't lasted much longer. The ambulance medics had tried to resuscitate him on the way to the hospital, but without success. When the car had rolled, he'd sustained head injuries that meant that even if they had managed to generate a pulse, it was unlikely he would regain consciousness.

Dani hadn't been judged to be at fault. The accident had happened on a narrow dirt road that was closer to one lane than two. There had been little room to manoeuvre, but even so, she had never been able to accept the verdict.

She had been an experienced enough driver, but most of her driving had been done on city roads, and in her own small sedan—not Robert Galbraith's large automatic. At the time she had been feeling her way with the unfamiliar car and the road, which had recently had a new load of gravel spread on it. She had always believed that if either Robert or Susan had been behind the wheel, they would have managed the car and the slippery conditions better and so survived the crash. She wouldn't have lost her mother and Robert—who had been the closest thing to a father she had ever known—and her much younger half-brother, David, wouldn't have lost both his parents.

To compound her guilt, she knew that if Robert

Galbraith and her mother were still alive, Galbraith
Station wouldn't be in such a shaky financial position.

With the help of a hired hand, Bill Harris, and
Aunt Ellen, who had moved out of her townhouse
in Mason and into Galbraith, Dani had quit her phys-
iotherapist's job and taken over the running of the
farm while she sorted out the financial tangle of
Robert Galbraith's affairs.

Despite an outward appearance of wealth, neither
Susan nor Robert had had a lot of money to spare,
nor had ever imagined dying before their time—cer-
tainly not in a car accident on one of Jackson's
Ridge's sleepiest country roads. They'd had insurance but only enough to cover the short-term debt
owing on the property. Although it had been in the
Galbraith family for generations, it had become
heavily mortgaged through Robert's various business ventures.

The investment structure, which had been solid
while Robert was alive, had collapsed like a house of
cards when he died. A kiwifruit orchard he'd had
shares in had proved successful, but fluctuations in
the market had eaten away the slim profits, and without Robert at the helm, the operation had eventually
been sold at a small loss. The largest loss had occurred
in the most lucrative of Robert's enterprises and his
pet project: his horse breaking and training business.

A renowned horse breaker, Robert had had a
lengthy client list and had commanded high fees.
The business, which had started out on a shoestring

budget, had expanded rapidly. To cope with the demand, Susan had begun working full-time with the horses, and a large amount of investment capital had been sunk into building a set of stables and a covered training facility. While Robert had been alive the income had been steady and substantial, more than enough to cover the mortgage, but, within days of his death, the horses had been removed and the income had dried up.

The final nail in the coffin was an ostrich contract Robert had bought into just before he'd died—a deal which required the purchase of a bird a year for a further period of five years at an exorbitant fixed price. So far the venture had failed to make anything but a loss. The ostrich industry had folded, and prices for the birds and the products had plummeted, leaving investors with a financial lemon that continued to squeeze *them* dry. The contracts were cleverly executed and legally binding, creating a financial drag that tied investors into paying for birds that were more use in a zoo than on a farm. For years Dani and the group of investors had waited for the syndicate that had set up the farm to fold, so freeing them, but against the odds the ostrich facility continued.

The easy option would have been to sell off a parcel of land to cover the debts, but over the past few years Robert Galbraith had already sold off the maximum amount of land allowed under the local authority rules to help fund the costs of the new businesses—the farm could no longer be subdivided. Any debts now had to be met out of farm capital.

During Dani's first interview with the bank, the possibility of bankruptcy and a mortgagee sale had been suggested, but she had refused to give in to that option. Her reaction had been knee-jerk and fierce. In his will, Robert Galbraith had entrusted her not only with David's care, but with Galbraith Station, which had been left jointly to both her and David. If Robert and Susan had still been alive, Galbraith Station would have prospered not only in a business sense but as the warm hub of their family.

The fact that they had died and she had had a part in it haunted her. For years—a shadowy carryover from childhood—she had quietly kept a watch on Susan, Robert and David. The vigilance had been habitual and ingrained. Sometimes Susan had chided her about being overprotective, but she'd accepted the way Dani felt: they were her family, and doubly precious to her because of the past.

But no amount of checking on the people around her family or personally ensuring their safety had helped in the few seconds it had taken for Susan and Robert's lives to end. As hard as she'd tried, she'd been powerless to save them, but she was determined to help David—and to save Galbraith.

Pushing to her feet, Dani walked out into the dusty area in front of the barn and stared at the clear blue sky. The shadows were lengthening and the air had cooled slightly, but it was still unseasonably hot.

Brown hills, the texture of the grass like velvet with the low angle of the sun, rolled into the hazy distance. Diminished as the property was, it was still substantial enough to provide a good income—provided there was rain.

The drought couldn't have happened at a worse time. The slow death of Galbraith Station was excruciating. Sometimes she felt as if the place was sucking every last iota of strength and endurance from her.

Directly after the funeral, when the will had been read, she'd been surprised to discover shares in the station had been left to her, but once the financial situation was sorted out she would hand them over to David. He'd need every resource at his disposal to keep the property, let alone farm it, and once he'd completed his agricultural diploma, she meant to see that he got his chance.

Methodically, she checked the tractor's diesel tank and refilled it ready for the morning. With fingers that were annoyingly clumsy, she reversed the pouring spout on the diesel container, screwed on the lid, and stored it in the corner of the shed. Picking up a rag, she wiped her hands, nose automatically wrinkling at the strong smell of the diesel.

Blankly, she stared at her hands. Her fingers were long, the shape of her hands elegant. As hard as she'd tried she could never get comfortable with the acrid smells, or with what the oil and diesel did to her skin and nails. Every now and then she rebelled and put on a coat of nail polish, only to go through the anger/denial thing when the next day the colour gradually chipped, peeled or dissolved away. Lately, she'd stopped bothering. Like her life, her beauty regime was pared down to the basics.

Absently, she strolled back to the house, taking a circuitous route through the vegetable garden. On the way she stopped to pick a lettuce, sprigs of basil and several ripe tomatoes for dinner—the habit of never walking anywhere without a purpose ingrained.

A practical task or not, for long moments she simply soaked in the pleasure of the garden, her arms filled with salad vegetables, eyes half-closed as she listened to the sound of the wind sifting through the trees and the melodic whistle of tui birds.

A faint click, as if a door had just been softly closed, jerked her head around.

Frowning, she studied the corrugated iron back of the barn, which provided a wind-shelter for the garden. The main doors, which were around the other side, were open, and usually stayed open unless the weather was wet.

On Galbraith Station theft had never been a problem; it was too isolated for casual thievery and, in any case, Jackson's Ridge was hardly a breeding ground for criminals. The town itself was small and sleepy—a coastal hideaway that attracted a few regular holidaymakers each summer and little else. Added to that Galbraith Station was a good twenty-minute drive out of town on a dusty dirt road. Apart from the occasional boatload of picnickers who landed on the beach below the house, Dani was lucky to see a stranger. Consequently, the house and shed doors were seldom locked.

With a silent tread, she walked around the barn,

straining to listen and separate the sounds that were always there: the roar of the surf, the creak as one of the branches of the flame tree in the home paddock sawed against another, the metallic clank when the wind came from the southwest and lifted a loose piece of roofing iron on the barn. This one hadn't been a product of Mother Nature, it had been a definite click.

Her tension mounted as she examined dusty farm implements and a towering pile of hay, the spurt of fear wiping out almost two decades of a measured, safe existence, abruptly transporting her back to a time when every sound had been suspect. Nothing appeared to be missing or out of place, and there was no sign that anyone, or anything had been in the barn but dust, birds and maybe a few mice. Shaking her head, she skimmed the dark reaches of the barn.

Something flickered in the shadows. A split second later a dark form arrowed past her, narrowly missing her head. Dani ducked, adrenaline rocketing through her veins as tomatoes and herbs scattered on the dusty concrete floor.

Nesting swallows.

Letting out a breath, Dani eased the pressure on the lettuce, which was crushed against her chest, bent and retrieved a tomato. A second swallow dove down from the rafters, slicing close as it flew through the doors.

Automatically, her gaze followed the tiny bird as it arced into the sky then wheeled for another run into the barn. Grabbing the rest of the bruised toma-

toes and the basil, she retreated back out into the
sunlight.

"Okay, okay… I haven't disturbed your babies."

And nobody else had, either. The swallows were
aggressive. If anybody had been in the barn the birds
would have been in the air, flying, before she had
gotten there. The sound she'd heard must have been
either the birds or some small animal, perhaps a rat,
upsetting something.

Shrugging, she started toward the house. As she
reached the veranda the distinct sound of a car hitting potholes stopped her in her tracks. Opening the
screen door, she deposited the vegetables on the
bench and turned to see who her visitor was.

The car was shiny beige and unfamiliar. Frowning, she studied the sleek expensive lines. She was
used to cars pulling up at the clinic, which was further down the drive, but not this late. Clinic hours
were normally ten until three, which fitted in with
her work routine and suited clients who wanted to
make an appointment during their lunch break.

Dust rose in a cloud around the vehicle as she
walked to meet the visitor. After the scare just moments ago, she felt tense and a little jittery. It wasn't
likely that someone arriving at her front door in day-
light would give her trouble, but since Ellen had
died she'd become acutely aware of her vulnerability on the isolated farm.

Lifting a hand to shade her eyes, Dani studied the
man who climbed out from behind the wheel. He
was tall, dark and physically imposing, with the kind

of smooth good looks that would make most women look twice.

He was wearing a suit. Her stomach dropped. He wasn't a real estate agent, his car was too clean and he didn't have any advertising slapped on his number plate. That meant he had to be with one of the stock and station agents—or the bank.

As soon as she caught a whiff of the subtle expensive cologne he was wearing, she crossed off the stock and station agencies.

"Ms. Marlow?"

"That's right."

She didn't miss the quick, male once-over he gave her. Even in a small place like Jackson's Ridge, she had gotten used to that look long before she'd turned sixteen. Deliberately, she turned her head so he caught the scar on the right side of her jaw, the narrow slash courtesy of the accident. She generally found that took some of the icing off the cake. She might look a certain way, but that didn't mean she was.

He introduced himself as Roger Wells, the new branch manager of Jackson's Ridge's only bank and slipped a business card from his wallet. "Nice place you've got here."

Dani tucked the card in her jeans pocket and tried not to notice how grubby her fingers were despite the wipe with the rag. Machine oil took no prisoners. "It's been a lot nicer in the past."

Galbraith used to be a showplace, with a six-bedroom homestead and extensive gardens. Now the house was in need of a coat of paint and repairs to the roof and verandas, and the gardens needed a lot more care and energy than she could expend.

He shoved both hands in his pants pockets, going for the casual *GQ* look and achieving it. "I just took a drive down to the beach. The views are really something."

Dani's spine tightened. She hadn't heard a vehicle until just now, which wasn't surprising, because the Dinosaur made so much noise, but even so she should have heard him sooner. That meant he must have driven down one of the stock roads at the far end of the farm, turned onto the beach road then back up onto the plateau via another stock road, bypassing most of the driveway to the house. Lately she'd heard more than the usual traffic along the beach road, and some of it at night. Despite the fact that it was trespassing, normally she didn't worry about the unauthorised access, because occasionally locals liked to surf-cast off the beach, but with the syndicate people sniffing around, she was extra wary. "Jackson's Bay is beautiful."

Even that was a mild understatement: it was spectacular—lonely and a little wild—a long, smooth crescent that curved into the distance and took a big bite out of the local coastline. Lately, owing to the syndicate's interest in Jackson's Ridge, she'd been inundated with more than the usual amount of real estate agents, all wanting her and David to sell. "So what can I do for you, Mr. Wells?" As open and pleasant as Wells seemed, it was after six, the sun was setting, and she wasn't inclined to trust him.

White teeth gleamed. "This is just a quick call to introduce myself and let you know it's business as usual with the bank. I like to take a personal interest in my clients."

She just bet he did. Maybe she was being oversensitive, there was nothing in the statement to take offence at, but Roger Wells was a stark change from Harold Buckley, the previous manager. Mr. Buckley had been with the bank for as long as Dani could remember, and she'd liked him. In all those years, he had never once bothered to take a drive out to Galbraith, let alone take an uninvited tour of the property. If there was any business to be done, it had always been completed in his office during business hours.

Wells made a few bland observations about the severity of the drought and the state of the economy— nothing that Dani hadn't tortured herself with a thousand times over already—then finally got to what really interested him, Galbraith's stock numbers.

Setting her jaw, Dani reeled off the figures. A year ago that many head of cattle would have represented a slim, but comfortable return, but with the price of beef falling to a ten-year low, her profit margin was gone and Wells knew it. "Is there a problem with the bank financing farm mortgages? I hear Tom Stoddard's looking at selling up."

The blunt tactic didn't net a return. "The bank's commitment to farmers hasn't changed."

Dani kept her face expressionless. She'd seen the ad on T.V.—something about the "friendly bank."

From what she'd heard, lately, the Jackson's Ridge bank was as friendly as a rottweiler. They had squeezed Tom so tight his options were gone.

After a few more uncomfortable pleasantries, Wells climbed back into his car and drove away. Dani watched the plume of dust until it dissipated, any appetite she'd had gone. As bland and pleasant as Wells had been, he represented trouble. He might have been on her land uninvited, but technically he owned more of Galbraith Station than either she or her brother did.

Chapter 4

The following afternoon, after taking a trip into town to buy groceries, Dani strolled down to the waterfront and met Becca McKay at Jackson's Ridge's only café.

Becca was the same age as Dani—a tanned, willowy blonde who'd spent most of her life travelling. Five years ago she had landed in Jackson's Ridge for a summer and waited tables for Nola, until she'd been swept off her feet by one of the coast's pastoral barons.

The marriage had caught everyone in Jackson's Ridge cold. John McKay was twelve years older than Becca and a widower. To compound matters, Becca's boss, Nola, just happened to be one of John's sisters. Nola had had an amiable relationship with Becca until John had started turning up as a regular customer. Since then, she hadn't been able to hide her disapproval of the age difference, or her opinion that the marriage was doomed to failure—despite the fact that John and Becca now had two children, with a third on the way.

Becca chose a table outside under a shade sail and shot her a meaningful look. "I heard Carter's back."

Dani pulled out a chair, sat down and braced herself. She and Becca had been friends for years, but they had differing opinions about Carter. Despite Carter's reputation for being cool and elusive, Becca was certain he was prime husband material—for the right woman. "How did you find out?"

Becca draped a colourful fringed bag that matched the orange and pink stripes of her tank top over the back of her chair. "John had a face-to-face in the supermarket. Carter reached for a bottle of hot sauce—he was getting ketchup for the kids. How typical is that?"

Dani couldn't help thinking that when it came to John McKay it was very typical. He was a devoted husband and father and made no bones about the fact that his wife and children came first. "Be warned. Carter Rawlings is not my favourite topic."

"Then you're on your own, because the whole town's humming. Word is out that he's got to pop the question this time."

Dani studied the laminated menu. "He did make a proposition last time he was back, but it was more along the lines of a suggestion that it would be more convenient all around if I moved in with him. I don't recall that a ring was part of the deal."

Dani poured two glasses of water from the carafe on the table. There had been no moonlight, no bended knee, just pure practicality. She took a sip of water and tried to forget the moment. Carter had been on his way out the door; his bags packed, his orders and passport on his bedside table, with that cool, distant look in his gaze. As always, the exit was practiced and slick. Dani didn't like to dwell on how many women had been put through the exact same routine. Even in Jackson's Ridge Carter had a certain reputation, and he hadn't earned it by being caught up in emotion. She shrugged. "I wasn't interested. The way I saw it, it was all about convenience. His."

Becca frowned. "Are you sure it's finished? Don't forget, he's a *guy.* They think differently—food, sex, football, business—and not necessarily in that order."

The screen door flipped open as Nola walked toward them with a pad.

"Twelve months sure. Carter and I broke up when he left. We're finished."

Nola's expression went utterly blank. She was a dedicated lifetime member of the Carter Rawlings fan club. In her eyes he could do no wrong, whereas Dani did wrong on a regular basis—like now, for example.

Becca took one look at Nola's face and set the menu down. "We'll have two lattes while we figure out what else we want. Is that okay?"

Nola's notebook snapped closed.

Becca waited until she was out of earshot. "She's in shock."

"I can't think why. It's the third time it's happened."

Becca's expression was rueful. "Only the third? The moon would have to turn blue before Nola admitted she might have it wrong. Once she gets her teeth into an idea she hangs on like grim death. According to John she had a thing going with Walter Douglas from the butcher shop when they were at school. He ended up marrying someone else and Nola's refused to date since. That's *thirty-five years* on the shelf because she figures that someone else got her guy."

The screen door to the café flipped open as a couple left.

"Talking about male cheesecake…" Becca jerked her head to indicate Roger Wells, who was seated inside near the window then averted her gaze as he pushed his chair back and strolled toward the door. She rolled her eyes. "He's coming this way. Do I look married?"

"Becca, you're six months pregnant. He's got to figure that you've at least got a guy."

"I guess. Plus he's just been over the farm books. What he doesn't know about me isn't worth printing." With a grin, she patted her belly. "Did I tell you it's a girl? I had a scan on Monday. John's over the moon."

Roger Wells inclined his head. "Mrs. McKay, Dani."

Becca made a face. Dani killed any hint of a smile and kept her gaze fixed on the collar of Wells's pristine white shirt. He wasn't wearing a suit jacket today, and looked younger and a lot more casual than he had the previous evening. With an effort, Dani made polite conversation, but her replies were forced; Wells represented the bank. No matter how charming, she couldn't get past that fact, or the fear that missing that mortgage payment engendered. Besides, he was just a little too smooth-tongued for her liking.

Nola appeared at the screen door with a tray. Wells did the gentlemanly thing and opened the door then lifted a hand as he strolled back to the office.

Becca fanned herself. "Looks like you've got yourself an inside track there, girl. From what I hear, Wells is single, lonely *and* alone."

Nola set the tray on the table with a sharp tap. "Better not let Carter catch him chatting you up." She threw a dismissive glance at Wells's retreating back, her voice pitched loud enough to carry. "Man must have a death wish."

Dani's jaw clamped. "Carter and I are finished. We've been finished for months."

Nola's expression didn't flicker and Dani had to wonder if she'd even heard.

A latte was placed in front of Dani, a small star-shaped biscotti and a sachet of sugar placed neatly on the saucer. "Let's hope *he* knows that."

Becca lifted a brow. "If I were you, Nola, I'd start worrying about it when it becomes your business."

Nola's head swivelled. Her gaze settled on Becca like a pair of twin lasers, old issues bubbling to the surface. "All I'm saying is it's a shame that boy has to come back from almost being killed and find out his girlfriend lost interest while he was lying in a hospital bed."

Dani ripped open a sachet of sugar and emptied it into her cup. "Like I said before, we broke up before he left. And he'd been gone about eight months before he hit the hospital bed."

"Hmmph." Nola turned on her heel.

Becca let out a breath. "She didn't know that."

Dani shrugged. "Neither did I, until I talked to Gladys Hainey at the supermarket."

Becca lifted her cup and took a reflective sip. "I should have kept my mouth shut."

Dani lifted a brow. "But—?"

Becca grinned. "Uh-huh. Impossible."

Dani cradled her cup between her fingers, and transferred her gaze to the view. The small cove the town was built around was sheltered, with rock promontories at both ends, a pretty stretch of shelly beach and enough deep water that fishing boats could tie up at the jetty. "Better drink up before Nola comes back to clean the table. You might have forgotten who owns this café, but I haven't. Closing time could be any second."

"Talking about closing. I heard the Barclays' barn caught on fire last week. According to John, they lost a shed full of plant."

Dani tensed, the memory of the fire and the swiftness with which it had spread, eating through steel and timber, wasn't one she'd forget in a hurry. "I was there—for an appointment. The building was already ablaze when I drove in the gates. By the time the Fire Service got there it was too late, the building had burned to the ground. Luckily they're covered by insurance."

Twenty minutes later, John arrived to pick up Becca.

Becca eased to her feet, grimacing as she rubbed the small of her back. "Brunch. Next Sunday?"

"It's a date." Becca's leisurely brunches were legendary, and usually peopled with an eclectic, sometimes oddball mix of characters. Whenever an invitation was issued, Dani always turned up. If the food itself was plain, it was a certainty the company wouldn't be—and, as it happened, Becca was a fabulous cook. All the years she'd spent travelling hadn't been wasted. She spoke several languages and cooked with inventive gusto. It was one of the things Nola just didn't get about Becca—she didn't see the interesting woman behind the pretty face.

Dani finished her coffee, hitched the strap of her purse over her shoulder and walked back toward the supermarket where she'd parked the truck. As she passed the alley that led to the back of the café, she paused. She could smell smoke.

A fragment of blackened paper with a glowing orange edge swirled in the breeze. The wisps of smoke thickened. Frowning, she stared down the narrow, potholed lane, reluctant to trespass. Nola wouldn't thank her for poking around her property, but she couldn't just walk away without investigating. Not after what had happened to the Barclays' barn. From what she knew of the layout of the shops that fringed the beach and the conglomeration of houses and flats built behind them, the buildings were too close to allow for any activity like burning rubbish.

She started down the alley. Her pulse rate quickened as she rounded a corner and was pushed back by a hot gust of smoke. Flames roared out of a Dumpster set against the back wall of the café. The fire had already taken a hold of the old weatherboard building, licking hungrily upward and threatening to catch on the small adjacent carport where Nola's car was parked. The wind—a sea breeze— was blowing hard enough to muffle the crackle of the flames, and inside the café music was playing, which was probably why Nola hadn't noticed that her livelihood was about to go up in flames.

Retracing her steps, Dani pounded on the door that opened out onto a small delivery bay. When there was no answer, she pushed her way inside.

A young girl stacking a dishwasher was visible down a small, dim hallway. Her head jerked up, her expression indignant. "You can't come in here—"

"The back of the café is on fire."

The girl gaped at her. Heart pounding, Dani spotted an ancient fire alarm and hose jutting from the wall. Taking off a shoe, she broke the glass and threw the switch. An ear-splitting ringing filled the building as she began unwinding hose.

Nola stepped into view. Her face went white, then bright red. Flames were now visible at the back window.

Dani dragged the hose out the door and down the steps. The girl followed, dragging loose hose with her. Dani thrust the nozzle into the girl's hands. "Start hosing. I'll call emergency services."

Grabbing a cell phone from her purse, Dani began dialling, and in that moment Nola snapped into action.

"I'll call Walter direct. It'll be faster."

Snatching up the café phone, she made the call. Aside from owning the butcher shop, Walter Douglas was head of the Fire Service, and the fire station was situated right next door to his shop.

She jammed the receiver back on its rest then went to clear the restaurant. Seconds later, she had closed the doors and moved her car out onto the road, barely missing the fire truck as it turned into the narrow drive. Minutes later the fire was out.

Nola stared at the flooded, blackened mess of the Dumpster and the charred section of wall, her expression stark.

Walter poked at the oily residue floating in the water. "What was in there?"

"The usual. Food scraps, some plastic and paper rubbish. A few boxes."

"Smells like kerosene or one of those fancy fire-lighting gels."

Nola looked blank. "It can't be. I don't *have* either."

He leaned forward and examined the residue more closely. "If you didn't throw an accelerant in there, then someone else did."

Some of the blankness left Nola's expression. "I thought it must have been caused by a cigarette butt—"

Walter's expression was grim. "Do you know anyone in this town who'd be stupid enough to throw a cigarette butt into a Dumpster of rubbish?" With a curt command, he directed two men to check under the building in case anything was still smouldering.

Nola transferred her attention to the blackened corner of the carport. "I can't believe it was deliberate. Who would want to burn down my café?"

Walter eased off his helmet. "It's thirty-plus degrees. People do dumb things in the heat." He turned to Dani. "It's a good job you spotted the smoke. Another couple of minutes and the whole place would have gone up. These old shops don't have any fire-retardant materials in them. They might look pretty, but they're nothing but fuel."

Light pooled on Dani's desk, illuminating the piles of bank statements and bills piled on either side of the farm cashbook. No matter which way she added the figures, the end result was always the same: not enough.

With rising interest rates, the mortgage scraped the ceiling of her capability to repay, even if the farm was doing well, which it wasn't. The small nest egg of money Aunt Ellen had left was gone, soaked up in taxes and mortgage payments. Until the herd was sold the only cash flow came from the jobs she and David worked.

David, who was almost eighteen, was on the last year of his diploma. Aside from attending classes, he pumped gas and waited tables, sending back what money he could. Once he graduated, the financial pressure would ease and he would come back to take over the farm and Dani could concentrate on her physiotherapy practice.

Yawning, she closed the books, switched off the lamp and walked out to the kitchen to make a cup of chamomile tea. She would prefer tea or even hot chocolate, but on doctor's orders she had to avoid overstimulating herself. Ever since childhood, she'd had trouble with the night. Usually she slept, but too much sugar or caffeine this late and, physically exhausted or not, she would spend the night staring at the ceiling.

She'd never told the doctor—or anyone else—just why it was she got so tense, and she never would. No one in Jackson's Ridge knew a thing about the years she and Susan had spent on the run from a psycho ex-boyfriend, including Carter, and as far as she was concerned that was how it was going to stay. Her past was one secret she was determined would remain buried along with the unsettling knowledge of just who the stalker was likely to be.

Seconds later Dani poured boiling water into a mug, let a herbal teabag steep for a few seconds then carried the drink over to the kitchen table. As she breathed in the fragrant steam, a distant light drew her eye, and her stomach tensed.

She could see glimpses of Carter's house from the kitchen window, and his light was on, specifically, his bedroom light. Great. All she needed.

Carter was her closest neighbour—there was no getting away from that. The entrance to his driveway was some distance away, but the house itself was almost claustrophobically close, built, like the Galbraith house, to catch the stunning view across Jackson's Bay.

The Galbraiths and the Rawlingses had been neighbours forever. In the past, they'd been so close they had been like one large extended family. They'd shared Christmas, taking turns to host each other, and they'd pitched in with farm work. Dani had spent as much time in Carter's house, watching his mother bake cakes and preserve fruit, as she'd spent in this one, and Carter had been equally at home in the Galbraith house.

With careful sips she drank the tea and waited for Carter's light to go out. Minutes ticked by. A shadow flickered over the light as if Carter had just walked between the lamp and the window and with slow deliberation, Dani set the cup down. It was after ten, she should be dead on her feet; Carter should be tucked up in his bed fast asleep.

With jerky movements, she tipped the rest of the tea down the sink, rinsed the cup and slotted it into the dishwasher.

A quick shower later and she was changed for bed, wearing a cotton tank top and drawstring shorts, her teeth brushed. Picking up the book on her bedside table, she began to read, turned a page, then stared blankly at the words, aware that she didn't have a clue what she had just read. She also had a headache.

Setting the book down, she shoved the cotton sheet—which was all she could bear in the heat—off her legs and strode back out to the kitchen. She noticed Carter's light was off.

Forcing her jaw to unclench, she rummaged in the pantry for a couple of painkillers, drank them down with a glass of water, then dumped bags of flour and sugar on the counter, followed by a container of chocolate chips. The way she felt now, exhausted or not, she wouldn't sleep. She either needed to eat or to bake, and since she wasn't hungry, it had to be baking. There was something about the whole ritual that was calming. Maybe it was just a nostalgia thing, with the added bonus of being able to enjoy the results, although there was no way she could risk eating a brownie tonight. If tea could overstimulate her, chocolate would send her into orbit.

An hour later, perspiring from the heat radiating out of the oven, she slid a tray of brownies onto the counter and stepped out onto the veranda to cool down. It was almost midnight. The painkillers had done their work; her headache was gone and she even felt drowsy.

Winding her hair into a firmer knot on top of her head, she sat on the ancient wooden bench just outside the door and let the night air cool her skin.

There was no moon yet; apart from the faint glimmer of stars and behind her the light in the kitchen, the darkness was close to absolute. In the distance she could hear the soothing cadences of the sea, and all around the incessant sawing of cicadas and crickets. On cue a large, shiny black cricket hopped past her foot, attracted by the light streaming out of the kitchen door. Tipping her head back, Dani stared at the night sky and, without warning, slipped back into memories that should have been dimmed by time but were instead as sharp as ice-cold shards of broken glass.

Tensing, she sat up, every last vestige of drowsiness gone. She hadn't thought about the night *he* had come in the window and attacked Susan for years. The apprehension she'd felt while checking out the barn this afternoon had obviously triggered the memory, and she had to remember it *was* just a memory.

A cold shiver slid down her spine. He would have tried to follow them, that much she had never doubted. He had been relentless—but he had never found them. Between them, Dani and Susan had outsmarted him—shifting from town to town, city to city like ghosts, sometimes taking on assumed names, sometimes even changing the colour of their hair, because the red had been so distinctive.

A rustling, a distinct sound like a footfall jerked her head around.

Heart pounding, she stared in the direction of the barn. There was no breeze to explain either sound.

The air was still and heavy with condensation. The only way one of the trees or shrubs that clustered around the outbuildings could rustle was if something or someone had brushed against them. As likely as it was to be something rather than someone, she had to check.

With a smooth movement, she rose to her feet and slipped inside the screen door, closing it silently behind her. Grabbing the flashlight from the shelf in the mudroom, she inched the door open and eased outside and down the steps, holding her breath while she listened.

The sound of the insects seemed heightened as she crept toward the barn, a cacophony that filled her ears so that the harder she strained to listen, the less she heard. Feeling her way, she crept into the opening of the barn and flicked the flashlight on, swinging the beam in an arc and double-checking the corners. When she was satisfied the barn was empty, instead of walking back out the main doors, she used the small side door that opened out onto the dusty space between the barn and the implement shed.

Flashlight now flicked off, her hand closed around the handle. Holding her breath, she pushed the door open and stepped outside. Between the two buildings it was almost as pitch-black as the inside of the barn had been. Using the flashlight had been reassuring, but any night vision she'd had was gone.

Gingerly, she stepped forward. Hot pain shot up her shin. She stumbled off balance, the flashlight slipping from her fingers as she gripped her leg. The back of one hand brushed against rough metal, and she remembered the ancient, rusted tractor scoop that sat against the barn wall, almost buried in weeds.

A light shone directly into her eyes, almost stopping her heart.

"What are you doing here?"

Dani bit back an unladylike word when Carter swung the flashlight beam so that it illuminated the barn wall, washing them both in light. "I might ask you the same thing."

"I was outside on the porch when I thought I heard someone over here."

Her jaw clamped. "*I'm* over here."

"You were in the kitchen. The sound came from the barn."

Dani massaged her shin again and wondered if the pain would ever stop. "I thought you'd gone to bed."

She caught the speculative glance he gave her and suppressed another bad word. Now he knew she'd been checking on him.

He shrugged. "I couldn't sleep."

"Next time try taking a pill."

"I don't take sleep aids."

She should have been ready for that one. Aside from being a career soldier and a self-confessed adrenaline junkie, Carter was a medic. Nothing went into that high-octane body that wasn't scrutinized and judged pure.

Wincing, Dani retrieved her flashlight, flicked it on and examined the derelict scoop. It didn't stick out from the wall by much. If she hadn't been sneaking she would never have walked into it.

"Are you okay?"

"Fine." Apart from needing a tranquillizer and very possibly a tetanus shot. Trying to ignore the hot little coal of pain, Dani swung the light around and studied either end of the alley, examining the dark shapes of the trees, and what might possibly be lurking beneath them.

Carter walked to the end of the barn and stared out into the night. Something about his quietness made all the fine hairs at her nape stand on end. If Carter had heard something, there must have been—

"I can smell brownies."

She let out a breath and felt like beating her head against the side of the shed. "I've been baking. And before you ask, the answer is no and no."

The last thing she needed right now was to hear that sexy, faintly plaintive note in his voice. He knew what buttons to push; he knew what made her melt. If she said yes to the brownies he'd take that as encouragement, and right now she couldn't afford the extra stress. Added to that he knew she was vulnerable at night and he knew she didn't like being alone. The first time she had weakened and given in to the attraction that had simmered between them for years had been barely a week after Susan's and Robert's funerals. Carter had been there, his shoulder at the ready, and she had dropped into his bed like a ripe plum. "Go home, Carter. There's nothing for you here."

"Your choice."

"That's right." Her choice, and against all the odds it felt good to say no.

She hadn't realized she was so angry until now. She thought she'd had plenty of time to get over him. In a weird way it wasn't even fair to be angry, because it wasn't as if Carter hadn't ever told her what he was like. He had always been too restless for Jackson's Ridge. The challenge of Special Forces suited him better than farming or a settled relationship ever would. He couldn't commit, pure and simple and she wasn't exactly prime relationship material either.

He strode past her and checked the large gravel turnaround area in front of the barn, as matter-of-fact as if they'd been talking about the price of hay.

Gripping her flashlight, she followed him. One of the things that upset her most was the fact that she'd let herself fall in love with Carter in the first place when she'd always promised herself that she wouldn't, but it seemed that her body had always had a different agenda than her mind. From that first moment, she'd been attracted—cancel that, stunned practically speechless—and he'd known it. It had complicated her life. She'd had enough guilt and issues to deal with without buying into a relationship that was never going to work.

"I've done a circuit of the place and checked the sheds. There's no one parked down the road, and I couldn't see anyone on the beach. At a guess, you've probably got a stray dog or cat hanging around."

Carter turned on his heel, and headed for the once-worn track between the two houses. For the first time since he'd flicked on his flashlight she registered that he was limping.

Remorse tempered her anger. He'd come over because he'd thought there was a prowler, and if there had been one she would have been more than happy for his support.

A brief shudder ran down her spine. This afternoon she had thought someone was in the barn. "Carter, wait."

She could just glimpse the pale flash of his T-shirt, enough to see that he'd stopped. Before she could change her mind, she walked inside, wrapped warm brownies in foil and took them out to him.

For a minute she thought he wasn't going to accept the peace offering.

"Thanks."

Within seconds he had disappeared.

Rubbing her arms against the faint breeze from the ocean, she walked back inside, letting the screen door slap closed behind her. Somehow she'd travelled from towering anger to appeasement. Now she actually felt sorry for him.

And how typical that she had caved in and given him brownies. Somewhere, through all this mess, she had really hoped that she had learned to say no, and mean it.

Chapter 5

The sound of an engine starting pulled Dani out of a deep sleep. She blinked at the bright light pouring through her bedroom window. For the first time since Ellen had died she had slept through her alarm.

With jerky movements, she shoved out of bed, pulled on fresh underwear, jeans and a T-shirt and jammed her feet into sneakers. Pushing out through the French doors that opened onto the veranda, she strode over to the shed. Carter had already backed the tractor out.

"What do you think you're doing?"

He parked beside the open double doors of the barn. Leaving the engine on idle, he jumped down. "You said you had to let Bill go."

"That doesn't mean I need you to—"

"Forget it, Dani. We're neighbours."

Her jaw clenched as he disappeared inside the barn and began loading hay onto the trailer. Trust Carter to pull the neighbour thing.

Despite the fact that he was having trouble with his lateral movement and he had the limp to contend with, he made the backbreaking job look effortless. "You're still hurt. You should be taking it easy."

"I've had months to take it easy. I need to get back in shape."

Way number two to bamboozle her. "And this is training?"

He brushed dust and hay off his T-shirt. "You can pay me with treatments."

She crossed her arms over her chest. "I am not treating you."

He shrugged and climbed back into the driver's seat. "Then someone else will."

The tractor eased forward.

Deliberately, Dani stepped in front, blocking him. "You don't know where the cattle are."

Carter spun the wheel and drove around her. "The north-east paddocks. I had a look last night."

"Did you get *any* sleep?"

The sarcastic sting made him grin. "About as much as you, darlin'."

Dani's teeth ground together. She had forgotten how much he loved a fight. "You don't have the right to do this."

Dust rolled around her as Carter headed out of the

yard. "Oh very good, Dani, very mature and in control."

Next time she would go for a big hit, like issuing him with a trespass notice. That should really make him tremble. The only problem was that Carter and the local policeman, Pete Murdoch, weren't just major buddies, they were related—even if it was only by marriage to an aunt. Murdoch would probably sooner see her behind bars than upset his nephew.

An hour later, Dani manoeuvred the farm's four-wheel drive across an almost-dry riverbed and parked beside a pump house that was silvered with age and crusted with dried lichen. Carter feeding and shifting the cattle meant she had more time to carry out her regular system of checks on the water holes and the pumps that fed the troughs. Most of the troughs were low and one she'd driven past had actually gone dry, which was a bad sign.

As soon as she swung out of the truck she could hear the hum of the pump. The system was set up so that when the water fell to a certain level, the pump activated. She'd checked the previous day and the water level had been fine, but in this heat, moisture evaporated so fast it didn't take long for water levels to drop. The pump had probably been going all night trying to fill the dry trough. Since the pump appeared to still be working, the fact that no water was getting through meant that the intake pipe was no longer underwater. Stomach tight, she picked her way across rocks bleached a pale grey in the intense, dry heat and located the end of the pipe, which was out of the water and guzzling air.

If she didn't get water flowing through the pipes fast the pump would overheat and burn out, which would be a disaster. She couldn't afford the hundreds of dollars a new pump would cost, and if she couldn't get the system up and running, she would have to buy water in.

Frowning, she checked the lay of the pipe. Normally it ran in a straight line from the pump shed and was anchored in the deepest part of the river. Somehow, it had moved several metres, or—cancel that—it had *been* moved.

There had been no torrential flood of water through the riverbed to throw the pipe out, and no animals in this particular paddock since the last time she checked the pump just two days ago. For the pipe to have shifted position meant someone had deliberately pulled it out of the river, leaving the pump to burn out and her cattle to go thirsty.

Removing her boots and socks, she rolled up the legs of her jeans and stepped into the trickling flow, dragging the length of alkathene. When it was stretched to its limit, she pushed the pipe into the deepest part of the pool and fastened it in place with a couple of heavy rocks. Wading deeper into the water, she held her hand over the end of the pipe to check the suction, which was halting. The pump was operating, but air had gotten through the system and it had lost pressure.

Stepping out of the water, Dani wiped her hands down her jeans and grabbed the bike pump that was kept in the toolbox in the back of the truck. Minutes later, sweat dripping, she unscrewed the bike pump from the nozzle on the pump, flicked the pump switch back on and prayed. Water spat and gurgled; seconds later the high-pitched whine settled down to a hum. If the pump was damaged, she couldn't tell.

Letting out a breath, Dani checked the suction of the pipe in the water then pulled on her socks and boots and began walking the pipeline, checking for leakages. With the intense ultraviolet light in New Zealand, plastic didn't last long out in the open. Most of the line was buried to protect it, but it was exposed in places. If there was any damage, it usually occurred around the troughs where the pipe was out of the ground and being walked on by cows.

With relief she saw the first trough was filling. When it had reached capacity, water would automatically feed on to the next trough, and so on.

Flickering movement at the edge of her vision drew her attention away from the steady flow of water. A vague, indefinable tension filled her as she examined the dense grove of ancient puriri trees that marked the boundary.

A hawk launched from a high branch, wheeling overhead, and she shook her head. She was becoming neurotic—seeing shadows where none existed. Someone had tampered with her water system—she hesitated to use the word *sabotage,* because it had probably just been a kid's prank. School had been out for weeks now, although there was no family within close range that had children old enough to pull a prank like that. The Barclays were the closest, their boundary butted up against the southern end of Galbraith, but their house was several miles away. It wasn't likely their children would wander this far, or have the strength to dislodge the rocks that had held the pipeline in place.

Still tense, she examined the ridge of hills visible from the high pasture and the reason for her tension finally registered. She could smell smoke, and now she could see it, drifting along in the wind, coming from the direction of Tom Stoddard's farm.

Gaze fixed on the smoke, her stomach tight, she began walking toward it, keeping the blue-grey column in sight until she entered the grove of trees.

Dried leaves crackled underfoot, the sound explosive in the quiet grove. Beneath the canopy of trees the air was close and aromatic, the light dim. Massive trunks thrust upward out of drifts of leaves, branches thick with epiphytes and dripping with creepers, but despite the dense, enclosing foliage the smell of smoke was still strong.

Quickening her step, she hurried through the grove, wishing she had taken the time to go back and get her truck. It wasn't like Tom to burn rubbish at this time of year. He was an ex-member of the local Fire Service and normally ultra safety conscious. With grass and trees like tinder and the fire risk on extreme, he knew better than anyone that all fires were banned.

When she emerged from the trees her heart squeezed tight and she broke into run. It wasn't a rubbish fire, it was Tom's house.

Breath shoving in and out of her lungs, she climbed a fence, stumbled through a ditch then ducked low to get under an electric fence, careful to avoid the live wire. As she straightened she checked her jeans pocket for the cell phone she usually carried for emergencies. Her jaw clenched when she came up empty. Because she'd been in and out of the creek, she'd left her phone in the truck.

Dried seed heads and stalks whipped around her legs as she ran, impeding her. As she got closer she realized the house itself wasn't ablaze, but almost everything else was. The old stables at the rear were a pyre and smoke poured from the barn and garage. Adrenaline pumping, she unfastened a gate, pushed it wide and ran into the gravelled area in front of Tom's outbuildings. His truck was missing, which meant he was either out on the farm or in town.

Cutting across a small square of lawn, she tried the front door of Tom's cottage, which was locked. Seconds later she'd tried every other door and window; every one was locked tight enough to resist a siege.

Frustrated, she peered through the glass panel of the kitchen door. She could see the phone sitting on the kitchen counter.

Dani cast around, looking for something to break the glass. Grabbing one of the rocks that formed a neat edging along the path, she drew back her arm and threw it.

It bounced.

With a fluid movement, she retrieved the rock and brought it crashing down on the panel. Glass shattered in a web like the windscreen of a car. As forceful as she'd been, the hole she'd made was the size of a walnut.

She couldn't believe it. Tom had laminated glass in his kitchen door.

Lifting the rock, she hammered at the glass until she'd knocked out enough to reach through and unfasten the door, but precious minutes had passed. Seconds later, she had emergency services on the line.

Struggling to stay calm, she reported the fire and supplied the address, then clamped down on her impatience when the operator asked her to supply her own name and details and requested she stay on the line.

The slow tick of the clock seemed preternaturally loud as her gaze swung around the kitchen. She noticed that something red speckled the glittering shards of glass and the trail ran from the door to the counter. Blankly, she registered that the slow drip of blood came from her. A long, shallow cut ran along the inside of her wrist; she must have cut herself when she'd broken the panel.

The popping crackle as timbers exploded jerked her head around. Stomach tight, she stared out of Tom's tiny, pristine kitchen as a thick column of smoke darkened the sky. The steady roaring of the fire had increased until it drowned out the slow tick of the clock, and fear gripped her. It would take a fire crew a good ten to fifteen minutes to get out here, by then it could all be over. Fingers slippery with blood, she fumbled the receiver back on its rest, grabbed a tea towel to wrap her wrist, using her teeth to knot it tight as she ran to the barn. She had given the operator all the information required. There was no way she could just stand in Tom's kitchen and watch while his place went up in flames. She could at least try to save his tractor and after that, she would do what she could to save the house.

Oily black smoke billowed as she entered the barn, the heat almost driving her back. The tractor was easy to find. Tom was very precise in his habits—he always parked his tractor in the same place— backed in so that it faced the door. Eyes stinging, lungs aching from holding her breath, she pulled herself into the driver's seat and felt for the keys. Her fingers brushed metal already hot from the flames licking at the back wall of the barn. Her heart plummeted. The keys weren't in the ignition, which mean Tom must have them either hidden or hanging somewhere.

Dragging her shirt up around her mouth and nose, she sucked in a breath and almost choked as acrid air burned her throat. Coughing, she swung down from the tractor and made her way to the door. The smoke was so thick she was having trouble breathing, let alone seeing. A blast of heat sent her reeling, a split second later she stumbled outside just as a vehicle drove into the yard. She had a glimpse of Tom's nut-brown face and wispy grey hair as he reversed, gravel spitting, then she doubled up in a paroxysm of coughing.

A gnarled hand gripped her arm. "Are you okay?"

"I called emergency services then I tried to get the tractor. Couldn't find the key."

Tom's expression was grim. "I've got a spare."

"Tom, *wait*." Dani's heart clenched as the old man disappeared into the smoke. Tom was as tough as rawhide, but if he didn't come out soon, she was going in after him.

Seconds later, the stuttering rumble of a tractor starting was followed by the dull gleam of smoke-blackened metal as Tom, equally blackened, drove his tractor, with a trailer hitched behind, out of the barn.

As Tom parked the tractor beside the truck in the paddock, a vehicle slid to a halt, gravel spraying.

Carter.

His gaze touched on hers, cold and brief as he swung out of the truck, then shifted to Tom. "Got sick of the old place, Tom?"

Coughing and clutching at his chest, Tom swung down from the tractor. "Someone has. Don't know how a fire could start in the stables. There's nothing in there." Wiping at streaming eyes, he reached for one of several shovels lying in the bed of the trailer and passed one to Carter. "Damned if it'll get the house, though—or start a bush fire."

"You still got that floating pump?"

"It's in the implement shed. I was going to get that next."

"I'll get it. If we drop it in the stream behind your house, we'll be able to spray down the back of the barn." His gaze switched to Dani. "You help Tom wet down the house with the garden hose." His meaning was clear: if they didn't stop Tom, he would keep going back into the sheds to rescue items.

Within minutes of locating the hose and directing a steady stream of water at the side of the house closest to the blaze, Dani heard a siren. Seconds later the fire truck pulled into the parking area in front of the barn, followed by two smaller trucks. From the logos on the vehicles, they were forestry crews driving "smoke chasers"—trucks with light appliances on the back that could go off road. When a fire was reported, not only the Fire Service but any company with a forestry interest within a certain radius were obliged to attend. In a rural community like Jackson's Ridge the fire-response teams were finely tuned, and lately, with the tinder-dry weather, they'd had to be. It was in everyone's best interests to get to a fire early.

Within seconds a steady stream of water was being pumped into the heart of the fire. The garden hose now superfluous, Dani went to help Carter with the floating pump.

Carter was thigh-deep in the stream, fastening the hose to the pump. The coupling secure, he backed out of the water. The pump was designed to float and suck water up from an intake at its base, which made it ideal as a portable fire-fighting tool, although it was of more use refilling the water tanks of fire appliances than for spraying the actual fire.

Dani uncoiled the length of hose sitting at the top of the bank, laying it out in a straight line pointing directly at the back of the barn. Retracing her steps, she picked up the end of the hose and hauled it down the bank, slipping and sliding in the mud and shale. As she passed the metal coupling to Carter, her sleeve peeled back from the makeshift bandage.

Carter's attention shifted to her arm. The towel was soaked red in places.

"What have you done to your wrist?"

"It's just a scratch."

"Not with that much blood." With deft movements, Carter checked that the coupling was locked on tight, waded into the middle of the stream and yanked the cord on the pump.

Blue smoke filled the air. The racket of the pump made any further conversation impossible. Pulling her sleeve down to cover the bandage, Dani climbed out of the muddy stream, her boots squelching.

One of the forestry crew was standing with the hose, legs braced as water fountained. Dani recognized the faces of the men helping: amongst them Walter Douglas and Jim McCarthy, both of whom had been volunteer firemen forever, and Athol Pike, the foreman for one of the major forestry companies. Her stomach automatically tensed when she recognized George Lynch, a regular holiday resident who owned a bach on the waterfront. He had been at the wheel of the furniture removal truck she had hit six years ago. Because the cab had been up so high, he'd only received minor injuries, but he'd still had to spend a night in the hospital.

A dark-haired man in jeans and a T-shirt stood out from the ranks of fire fighters and forestry workers, all of whom were dressed in coveralls.

The crumping sound of an explosion jerked Dani's head around.

Tom's expression was stoic. "There goes the drum of petrol. Now there'll be no stopping it."

"If the petrol's only just gone, that means it wasn't used to light it."

Dani stared at the stranger, who looked vaguely familiar. She'd heard an out-of-towner was staying in the Hamilton holiday cottage, which bordered her land. There were no prizes for guessing it was him, but after the spooky incidents around the farm, the sabotage and the fact that this was the third fire in Jackson's Ridge within a week, her tolerance for strangers was low. "What makes you think the fire was deliberate?"

He shrugged, his expression non-committal. "It's not the first one in Jackson's Ridge."

Chapter 6

Within half an hour the fire was doused, and hot spots that had flared up in the paddock had been dampened down. The wife of one of the fire fighters had arrived with a cooler filled with bottled water, a large thermos of tea, and sandwiches.

Carter appeared beside Dani with a bottle of water, his expression grim. "Give me a look at your arm."

She stared at the sipper bottle, her mouth suddenly bone-dry. "It's just a scratch."

He handed her the bottle. "Trade."

"Not fair."

"When was I ever?" He indicated the bed of his truck, which had the tailgate down. "You'll need to sit down."

Perching on the back of the truck, she allowed him to unknot the towel and examine the cut, averting her gaze when she saw the livid slash. Call her squeamish, but she didn't like blood: too many bad memories.

If she was squeamish, Carter wasn't. He could have been looking at a mosquito bite for all the emotion he showed. "At least it's clean."

She took a long swallow of water and almost sighed with pleasure. "It ought to be, I bled enough."

"How much?"

He opened a case and extracted a bottle. Liquid stung like cold fire.

"Ouch. I don't know—I was busy."

He dabbed at the cut with more of the nasty stuff. She flinched.

"Keep still. You could do with a couple of stitches at your wrist—you've just missed nicking an artery. How did you do it?"

"I had to do a little B and E to get to Tom's phone. I didn't expect the glass in his kitchen door to be laminated."

He relinquished his grip. Something shiny glinted.

"What is *that?* A *needle?*"

He gripped her wrist. "Don't be a baby."

Oh great. Anesthetic. Her eyes squeezed shut. "This is not a battlefield, Carter, and I am not— *ouch*—a pincushion."

He dropped the disposable needle in the case and picked up another one, this one with a small, wicked curve. "If I don't put a stitch in now, you'll have to drive in to the medical centre. Either way you're going to have a scar."

He threaded the small needle. She lowered the water bottle, feeling faintly dizzy. "It'll add to the collection."

One on her jaw, a jagged trail down her torso all the way to her hip, and a criss-cross series down the inside of one arm where she'd instinctively thrown it up to shield her face from the shattering windscreen.

"Are you all right?"

"Just give me a minute. I'll feel better when it's bandaged."

Blinking against another wave of dizziness, she concentrated on the fire crew rolling up hose. As Carter worked, the cacophony of throbs and stings gradually melted away as the numbness spread. She felt exhausted and a little bleary, the aftermath of adrenaline and shock.

Carter handed her wrist back, now thickly padded with a bandage. She pulled her sleeve down, avoiding his gaze. "Thanks."

"No problem."

She watched as Carter began treating the stranger, who had a nasty burn on the back of his hand. Carter had his own share of scars. Unfortunately, she remembered every one. Almost. She hadn't seen his latest scar, which, according to local gossip, had almost killed him.

A police cruiser pulled in and took a parking

space beside Carter's four-wheel drive, closely followed by a sporty hatchback that Dani recognized as belonging to Tony Flynn, the owner and lone reporter of the local newspaper, the *Jackson's Ridge Chronicle.*

Pete Murdoch eased out from behind the wheel of the cruiser, a black notebook in his hand. After briefly surveying the scene, he walked over to Tom, who was sitting, exhausted, beside the fire chief. Minutes later, Murdoch approached Dani.

"Tom says you were first on the scene."

"That's right."

"Where's your vehicle?"

She jerked her thumb in the general direction of Galbraith Station. "Parked back at the pump shed."

"So you walked here?" His voice held a faintly incredulous note.

"Ran, actually. As soon as I saw smoke."

"You put the call in from Tom's house. Why didn't you use your cell phone?"

Alarm prickled at the back of her neck. Murdoch's questioning was businesslike and definitely cool, with a faint edge that was confusing. "I was in and out of the river and walking my water line, my cell phone was back in the truck. I didn't go back for the truck because I was already halfway here when I saw the smoke."

She took another swallow of water, her unease expanding when Flynn moved within hearing distance, his pen and notebook out. Seconds later, Carter propped himself against the truck, the move seemingly casual, but successfully cutting Flynn out of the conversation.

"I don't get where you're going with this," she said, although she was beginning to. "I got here as fast as I could. Maybe I could have gotten here faster in the truck, but given that I would have had to have driven out onto the road before turning into Tom's drive, I don't think so. When I got here, I had to break into Tom's house to call emergency services. Tom arrived shortly afterward."

Murdoch made notes. "Just seems odd to me that you arrived at your next-door neighbour's fire with no vehicle and no phone on you."

"Are you trying to say I didn't want to help?"

"I'm not saying anything at all. I'm just trying to establish exactly what happened and when."

Carter's expression was stony. "What Murdoch's getting at is that perpetrators like to revisit the scene of the crime as a little extra insurance because it means if their prints or DNA are found, they can claim it was from the later visit—and bang, there goes the case."

Murdoch shot Carter an irritated look.

Dani stared at Murdoch in disbelief. She had known him for six years. He had been one of the officers who had attended the accident that had killed her mother and Robert Galbraith. He had been present at the inquest, and had always gone out of his way to check on her and make sure she was okay. "I didn't start the fire."

"Calm down. I'm not saying—"

"Yes. You are." Incensed, she shot to her feet and shoved the water bottle at Carter. "If I'm your best suspect, Jackson's Ridge is in trouble. What about Flynn, or Pike—or *him?* He's not connected with the crews."

Murdoch glanced at the stranger Carter had just treated. "Never mind about O'Halloran."

O'Halloran glanced up, his expression bland. "She's right. Look for your suspects elsewhere, she's not the type."

A nerve at the side of Murdoch's jaw jumped. "I don't want trouble from you, O'Halloran."

The man straightened from the bumper of the vehicle he'd been leaning on. "I'm not planning any."

Dani stared at O'Halloran. "If you're not local and you're not part of the fire crews, just what *are* you doing here?"

O'Halloran pulled his gaze from the smoking ruin of the stables and the charred exterior of the barn. "Actually, I came looking for you. I'm your ten o'clock appointment."

A few minutes later the fire truck and all but one of the forestry crews, which was staying on mop-up duty for the rest of the day, pulled out. Tony Flynn had left, hot on Murdoch's tail—his nose practically twitching with excitement.

Tom's sister, who owned a small beach house in town, arrived to stay with Tom, who was looking pale and shattered beneath the soot that streaked his face.

Satisfied that Tom was in good hands, Dani began walking across the paddock, heading for her truck and home.

Carter stepped in her path. "I'm giving you a lift."

"I don't need one. My truck's down by the pump house."

"You're not walking."

Dani made a production of looking down at her legs. "Could have fooled me." She noticed that aside from being wet and muddy, her jeans were blackened with smoke and soot, which meant she looked like almost everyone else—as if she'd been dragged backward through a chimney. A short, muscular man, dressed in forestry coveralls lifted a brow. "You two fallen out?"

Irritated, Dani glanced at Athol Pike, who was loading hose along with another member of the forestry gang, Eddie Thompson. Dani had been at school with both men, although Athol was a couple of years older. "That's none of your business."

White teeth gleamed. "Does that mean I finally get a date?"

Eddie snickered.

Carter's expression didn't change, but something about him must have made Pike feel a chill. He held up both hands, all sign of humour gone. "I was only kidding."

Dani glanced at Carter. First he had practically stood over Murdoch while he questioned her, now he was warning Pike off. "Does that mean you're turning me down, Athol?"

Carter snapped the tailgate of his truck closed.

O'Halloran looked interested. "I can give you a lift."

A shovel hit the bed of Carter's truck. "She's not treating you today."

O'Halloran turned his attention to Carter. "I didn't expect her to."

Dani finally made direct eye contact with Carter and almost flinched. Now she knew why Pike had backed down. "It's rude to talk about people in the third person when they're still present."

Carter opened the passenger door. "Get in the truck, Dani. You need to go home."

That was true. She still felt faintly dizzy, which was a bad sign. She could make it to her truck on foot, but she had a feeling she might need to lie down and rest before she got there.

Pike and Thompson had melted away. She glanced at O'Halloran, who looked as though he had a stubborn streak. "Will ten o'clock tomorrow do?"

His gaze dropped to her wrist. "Are you sure you're up to it?"

Dani flexed her fingers. The anaesthetic had numbed the area, but even so she could still feel a throb. "From memory, your doctor referred you for a neck and shoulder problem."

"That's right. A beam dropped across my back."

She recalled the notes Jan Pearce, an orthopaedic specialist from Auckland, had faxed her. The beam had crushed one shoulder and broken his neck. He had been lucky to survive the accident, let alone come out of it functioning normally. He'd come through surgery and months of physiotherapy with flying colours. All he required from her was a little maintenance work while he was on holiday. She blinked, her head heavy, as if a vice was slowly tightening on her skull. "How did that happen?"

O'Halloran turned away. "In a fire."

A hand curled around her upper arm, the touch electric even through the cotton of her T-shirt. "In," Carter snapped. "Before you pass out."

Dani jerked free. "I'm not going to faint." She hauled herself into the passenger seat and clung to the dash. "I never faint."

The door closed with an expensive thunk. Carter didn't bother arguing.

Minutes later, Carter pulled up beside her house. After nearly falling asleep while he drove, Dani didn't protest when he walked around the vehicle, opened her door and helped her down. Her head was one solid ache; any movement was painful.

Hanging onto the railing she pulled herself up the steps to the kitchen door, one step at a time, levered off her boots and socks and walked into the kitchen.

"Go and lie down, I'll bring you some painkillers."

Dani clung to the counter. "You're not coming into my bedroom."

She caught a hint of frustration in his expression. "Then lie on the couch."

Moving slowly, Dani walked down the hallway and grabbed a couple of towels from the linen cupboard, then spread the towels over an ancient, well-padded sofa so she wouldn't stain it with her sooty clothes. With a sigh, she stretched out.

Carter handed her two pills and a large glass of water. "You're probably dehydrated. When you've finished the water I'll get you some more."

After drinking a second glass, Dani eased herself into a more comfortable position and let herself drift. She could hear Carter out in the kitchen washing the glass. After her initial reaction against letting him into her personal space, it was oddly comforting to have him in the house.

Maybe *comfort* was a strange word to use, but Dani couldn't think of a better way to describe how she felt. Carter had a knack for taking control of situations and bringing order to chaos. It was a quality that carried its own attraction. Today he'd steadied Tom and looked after her—suturing her cut and buffering her from Murdoch's questioning and Flynn's acid pen. If Carter hadn't been there, casually staking a claim on her, she was almost certain Murdoch would have gone further—maybe even taken her in for questioning.

It was a fact that everyone in town still assumed she was Carter's girl—despite her assertion that she wasn't. The reality of still being under his protection was difficult.

In ten years' time—maybe—it would be funny....

A faint sound, the soft weight of a blanket on her

legs jerked her awake and for a moment she had trouble orienting herself. She felt as though she'd been asleep for hours, but she must have drifted off for only a few seconds.

Carter bent and tucked the blanket in against the rear of the sofa so it wouldn't slide off if she moved. The back of his hand brushed her fingers. The contact was fleeting, but the look that went with it—a moment of softness, of *recognition*—was intimate enough to curl her toes.

Seconds later the room was empty again. She heard the click of the front door closing and, shortly after, the receding sound of his truck as he drove down the drive.

Her fingers curled into the feather-light mohair rug. She still felt faintly dizzy, but now her mind was alive with memories of nights spent curled up with Carter, and long, lazy afternoons on the beach.

Why did he have to do that?

She had been *over* him.

Shoving to her feet, she made her way to the shower.

Now, exhausted or not, she was going to have trouble sleeping.

Carter walked into his kitchen and tensed. The tall, tanned figure standing at his kitchen bench pouring ice water into a tall glass was instantly recognizable.

"Mia."

She grinned and winked. "Hey! Don't sound so

pleased to see me. I was picking fruit down this way and decided to run you to ground. You're a hard man to find—I had to ask for directions at the general store. Someone named Gladys told me how to find you." She hooked a chair out from the table and sat down. "It is a general store, isn't it? Definitely not a supermarket—Jackson's Ridge has to be one of the smallest towns I've ever seen."

Carter fixed on the one point that seemed salient. "You asked at the general store?" That meant that by now everyone in town would know he had a female visitor. Jackson's Ridge might be tiny, but it had a communications network—code name, Gladys Hainey—that made satellite coms look primitive. If Gladys ever donated her body to medical science, worldwide intelligence would take a quantum leap.

"Uh-huh. And the pub, but the lady at the store was a little more forthcoming."

Mia sipped her water and nibbled at a salad roll. Carter stifled a groan. That meant she'd also been to the café.

"Oh, here, I brought you one!" She handed him a paper bag with a roll inside. "You know me. Cooking isn't my best talent."

His memory was a little fuzzy on that point, but no, it hadn't been.

Despite the name, there was nothing small and cute about Mia. She was lean and muscled, and just under six feet tall. Carter had met her at his local gym where she worked as a personal trainer and took aerobic classes in her spare time.

With a shrug, he took a chair and made a start on the salad roll. Amazon status or not, Mia was as friendly as a puppy and as harmless, and there was nothing he could do about her now. "What's with the fruit picking?"

"Thought it was a good way to do some travelling and catch up with friends. When I'm finished with the strawberries, I'm on my way down to Nelson to pick apples."

She jerked her head in the direction of a pack propped against the ancient Welsh dresser that took up most of one of the kitchen walls. "You don't mind if I stay the night, do you? I tried to get a room at the pub, but they're all booked. Apparently some loon's trying to burn out one of the local farmers and they're having to put up extra fire crew and cops." She gave him an amused look. "Which would explain why you look like a chimney sweep."

"And smell like one. The fire was at a neighbour's. He lost his stables."

Mia looked blank. Nice as she was, she was a city girl. Her reality had always been a whole lot different to his.

She indicated a bag of groceries on the counter. "I bought food."

"No problem." Carter studied the groceries with resignation. Kicking her out was an attractive proposition, but not viable if she didn't have anywhere else to stay. He'd known Mia for years, and he'd slept on her couch a couple of times after they'd broken up.

"I've put my foot in it. I thought I was getting some weird looks in town." She set her roll down. "You've got a girlfriend."

"Not exactly." He had an ex-girlfriend, and she was going to kill him.

"Don't worry, I'll be gone in the morning. First thing."

Silence reigned while she took another bite of her roll, chewed and swallowed. She gave Carter a reflective look. "You know, I've often thought you should have been the one."

Carter could feel his mind going slightly crazy. It was the reason that whatever he and Mia had shared had been brief. He frowned. "The one?"

"You know. The *one*." She shrugged. "I don't know why it didn't work out. You're perfect for me."

Carter stepped out of the shower, pulled on some fresh clothes then walked out to the kitchen. He picked up the portable phone, carried it out onto the veranda and dialled.

Murdoch picked up on the second ring.

Carter bypassed the pleasantries. "Who's O'Halloran?"

"Why do you want to know?"

"I like to know who my neighbours are." And something about O'Halloran niggled at him. He was familiar, but Carter couldn't place him, which was unusual.

"He's more Dani's neighbour than yours. He's staying at that beach house at the edge of her property."

"The Hamilton place?"

"That's it. He was married to one of the daughters."

Carter stared at the beach, at the creamy line of surf and the long, glassy stretch of wet sand as the water sucked back for the next wave. "What's he doing here?"

"Having a holiday, I guess. It is summer."

"You don't know anything else?"

"Why would I?" Murdoch sounded distinctly cagey.

Carter kept his tone mild. "Looked to me like you knew him."

"Like I said, he was married to one of the Hamilton girls. I've seen him around."

Which was more than Carter had. After exchanging a few pleasantries and asking after his aunt, Carter set the phone down. He stared at the waves coming in in sets. Something was going on in Jackson's Ridge—something that was giving him a cold itch down his spine, and Murdoch knew a lot more than he was admitting to.

Chapter 7

Sunlight on her face woke Dani. Pushing to her feet, she made her way to the bathroom and examined herself in the mirror. Aside from the bandage on her wrist she looked surprisingly normal. Despite the emotional turmoil, she'd actually managed to sleep in.

Thirty minutes later, showered and changed into her work clothes, she walked out to the barn. She'd heard the tractor just minutes ago. It was now parked back in the shed, which meant Carter had beat her to the punch again and had already fed out.

Now at a loose end, she retraced her steps to the kitchen and poured herself another cup of tea. She was trying hard to find things not to like about Carter—and failing. Despite everything he was turning out to be a proverbial tower of strength. He'd helped save Tom's place, patched everyone up, including her, and he'd stepped in to help her on the farm, taking on the most physical job. The fact that he'd slipped back into the farm routine so easily reminded her that while Carter might be a soldier by choice, he had always been a skilled farmer.

The least she could do was take him some more brownies. She would leave them on his kitchen counter.

Holding a plate of brownies covered in plastic wrap in one hand, she knocked then opened his front door and stopped dead.

The woman was tall and built like a Paris runway model and, in a skimpy bikini and see-through sarong, close to naked.

She finished winding a satiny swathe of black hair in a knot on top of her head. "Carter's outside somewhere. Do you want me to call him?"

"No. Thank you." Inconsequentially, Dani noticed that the strange woman was posed alongside an oil painting of Carter's great-great-grandmother. Amalie Rawlings had been tall and dark and gorgeous—a lot like the stranger. According to Rawlings family legend she had been engaged to an aristocrat but had abandoned a titled husband in favour of Thomas Rawlings—a reformed rake. In deep disfavour, Thomas had left England and carried off his bride. Amalie and her husband had settled in Jackson's Bay at about the same time the Galbraith family had.

Jaw set, Dani turned on her heel and started down the steps. Seeing the dark woman standing next to Amalie had put her relationship with Carter right back in perspective. Thomas Rawlings had given up king and country for Amalie, and she had had the ring to prove it.

"Wait! It's not what you think."

Dani pasted a smile on her face. "I don't think anything. I'm just his neighbour."

As she walked down the front steps, she caught a glimpse of Carter out in the paddock, his shirt off, sweat gleaming on his broad shoulders as he repaired a fence and for a disorienting moment her carefully constructed reality wobbled and shifted. The scene was a practical everyday one, but the emotions it engendered weren't.

Dani's fingers tightened on the plate. She felt as if a set of blinkers had just been ripped off. Injured or not, Carter was tough and fit with a methodical patience that was formidable. She had heard the bare details of what had happened to him in Indonesia, of how he'd survived months in captivity and a potentially lethal wound through skill and sheer endurance, not only engineering his own escape, but tracking the team that had been sent to rescue him until *he* found *them.* For years she had tried to slot him into a controllable compartment in her life, but the system hadn't worked because of two fundamental flaws.

A, he wasn't controllable, and *B*, she was in love with him.

Abruptly she understood what had happened to her mother when she'd met Galbraith, and every other woman who had ever fallen in love. The emotions were swamping, invasive and utterly logical. She wanted, she needed and she had to have.

The second she had seen the dark-haired woman in Carter's house, a primitive female part of her had gone ballistic. The emotions bordered on savage; she had wanted to drag her out by the hair. She couldn't tolerate the woman in Carter's house for the simple reason that Carter was *hers.*

She had said she was "just his neighbour" but she didn't want to be "just" anything to Carter. The magnitude of what she wanted was stunning—especially in view of the fact that she had lost him.

A popping sound jerked her gaze down. Her thumb had punctured the plastic wrap. She loosened her grip and stared at the brownies.

Aside from having her world tipped upside down, she was definitely going soft in the head. Actually taking Carter chocolate. The next thing she'd be crawling into his bed.

If there was room.

An hour later, pale and barely composed, Dani was dressed for the clinic in track pants and a T-shirt, her hair pulled back in a ponytail. As she walked across the front lawn, Carter detached himself from the shaded side of the barn and fell into step beside her.

Dani controlled the urge to speed up. For the first

time in years she wasn't just aware of Carter, she was suffocatingly aware of herself: the way her pulse jumped up a notch when he was near, the acute sensitivity of her skin.

She needed time to think—time to adjust. She needed time to form a strategy that would keep her sane and safe. In this case the solution of packing her bags and running didn't apply. Galbraith Station had her in a stranglehold: like it or not, she had to stay.

A flicker of movement through the trees drew Dani's gaze. The dark-haired woman was loading a pack onto the back of Carter's truck.

Grimly, she avoided looking at Carter. "You'd better go. Looks like your girlfriend wants to leave."

He said something low beneath his breath. "Mia's not my girlfriend."

"Mia?" Even her name was exotic. Dani felt like banging her head against something hard. Why on earth had she thought finishing with Carter would be some kind of punishment for him? If there had ever been an emotional vacuum in his life it must have lasted all of two seconds. She'd always known there was a queue—now it looked like it was starting at the farm gate.

Long brown fingers closed around her arm sending a hard jolt of heat through her. "I don't want Mia, I never have. I want you."

Carter's gaze was steady, focused with a male intensity that sent a raw shiver through her, and not for the first time she recognized the dominant male qualities that should have sent her running.

It was ironic that after the trauma of her childhood, she should choose a man who was by his own admission dangerous, but maybe that, more than anything else, made sense. After years on the run she was never going to be attracted to a weakling and Carter had succeeded in a field that broke strong men. He wasn't the hunted, as she and Susan had been. He was the hunter.

With careful precision she released herself from his hold. Somehow this had all gotten way out of control.

Yesterday their relationship had been over; now she didn't know what they had. She had stepped out of her comfort zone into alien territory, and when it came to dealing with Carter, control had always been important. As strong as she was, he had always been in danger of overwhelming her. As much as Dani had given, he had wanted more, and the instinct to protect herself was too ingrained for her to surrender easily.

"If she's not your girlfriend, why is she staying with you?"

He glanced at his truck, his expression frustrated. Mia had the tailgate down and was perched on the end of the tray, enjoying the sun. "If I knew the answer to that, I'd tell you. She was there when I got back from the fire yesterday. Look, we need to talk—"

The sound of a vehicle engine preceded the plume of dust as O'Halloran's truck rounded the corner and pulled into the small parking area in front of her clinic. Dani checked her watch. It was ten on the dot; whatever else O'Halloran might or might not be he was punctual, his timing impeccable.

Dani covered the last few paces to the building and shoved the key in the lock. Carter pushed the door open and stepped into the clinic ahead of her.

Reaching up, she slipped the key on the hook just inside the door. "What do you think you're doing?"

"In case you hadn't heard, there's an arsonist in town."

"In case *you* didn't hear, Murdoch thinks it's me."

Carter didn't bother to answer. Irritated, Dani pushed open windows. "So what? You think O'Halloran's the arsonist?"

"What I want to know is why Murdoch thinks it's you."

Dani felt heat build in her cheeks. She hadn't committed a crime, but having to repeat the reasons why Murdoch thought she might have made her feel guilty. She marched through to the reception area to unlock the front door. "Because I was first on the scene at the fire over at the Barclays' place, and I also happened to be in town when Nola had her fire."

First on the scene again.

O'Halloran stepped through the door. Without the covering of ash and soot, he was younger than she'd thought—early thirties at the most—with the dark tan and muscular build of someone who spent a lot of time working outdoors. For a man who had almost died eighteen months ago, he looked remarkably fit and well.

His gaze settled on Carter. The temperature in the room dropped by a few degrees.

Dani gestured him through to the treatment room and threw Carter a meaningful glance. Carter picked up a magazine and sat down in one of the easy chairs, his message clear.

He wasn't leaving until O'Halloran left.

At three-thirty Dani deposited the day's earnings in at the Jackson's Ridge bank and requested a balance on the farm account.

Her earnings had bolstered the account, but only marginally. She would have to empty the chequing account to pay the ostrich bill. Once that debt was cleared, she and David would be flat broke.

Half an hour later, she walked into the house, picked up the phone and dialled David's number. After fielding joking comments from two of his flat-mates, she finally got David.

"I'm going to sell some furniture."

There was a short silence. "Don't do that. I'll sell the car, it's got no sentimental value."

That was typical David. Ever since he'd been small he'd had a sharp, clear intelligence, and despite his relative youth he had a flair for farming and business. It had been his decision to shift from sheep into beef that had finally turned the farm's finances around—until the drought had struck. David himself had no time for unnecessary luxuries; he would have sold the furniture in a second, but he knew *she* liked the furniture. "The furniture can go, you need a car."

"I'll catch a bus, or hitch a ride with a mate."

"I've already got a buyer."

"You won't get much," he said curtly. "Dad sold off the antiques that were worth anything years ago. Getting rid of the car makes sense, it costs more than it's worth to run. Besides, it's only a few weeks until exams then I'll be back for good. Once I'm home, I can use the truck. "

"You won't get much for the car."

"A few hundred dollars is better than nothing."

Dani set the phone down and studied the figures. Every time she added up what they had against what was owed, she felt sick. No matter how optimistic she tried to be, she couldn't beat the maths. Even if David sold the car and she sold every piece of furniture in the house, unless the price of beef lifted they would still be short.

Pushing back the chair, she walked through the big airy rooms of the house, finally stopping in the room that Robert Galbraith and her mother had shared.

She slid open one of the small top drawers of a dressing table and lifted out a battered wooden casket: her grandmother's jewels. She hadn't mentioned them to David, because if he knew she was selling them he would go crazy.

One by one she opened velvet-lined cases and draped the pretty jewels on the bedspread. Ever since she'd been a child she'd been fascinated by the flash and glitter: a delicate diamond brooch in the shape of a star, a crescent-shaped hair ornament that had once had egret feathers in it, strings of pearls that glowed with a rich bronze lustre and a Victorian posy ring glittering with tiny gems. The jewellery, valuable as it was, represented much more than a financial nest egg. The pieces were the only link she had to a family she had never been a part of, fragments from Susan's past, and another age—one that celebrated the importance of family and marriage—when the jewels a bride wore were passed down through generations. In Susan's case, as the sole remaining heir, she had been bequeathed the jewels when her mother had died shortly before Dani had been born.

Slipping the pieces back into the box, she walked out to the kitchen, looked up a number in the phone directory and picked up the phone. Seconds later a slightly cracked, no-nonsense voice answered. Harriet Dawson was in her seventies and ran an upmarket boutique jewellery business in the much larger neighbouring town of Mason. She had been a longtime friend of Aunt Ellen's and had insisted on the odd occasions that she had visited that Dani and David address her as Aunt Harriet. When Ellen had died, Harriet had told Dani to keep in touch and if she needed help to let her know. This wasn't quite the help Harriet had envisioned, but there was no way around the fact that the jewellery had to be sold.

Briefly, Dani described the pieces. "How long would it take to sell them?"

There was a long pause. "Are you sure you want to sell?"

"I wouldn't have rung if I wasn't sure."

"If they look as good as they sound, they would sell almost immediately. I have a number of collectors I buy for."

Dani's attention sharpened. "*You* wouldn't be buying them would you Aunt Harriet?"

She snorted. "What would I want more jewellery for? I spend all day looking at it and half the night worrying someone's stealing it. I hate to see you lose family treasures, but at least I can make sure you get what they're worth."

Chapter 8

The gates of the ostrich facility gleamed in the late-afternoon sunlight as Dani drove in and parked beside the office and shop. Harry Tapp eventually emerged from the building, his grey hair rumpled, eyes bleary as if he'd just woken from a nap, which was probably the case. He was known to be shy of sunlight and nocturnal in his habits—notably at the bar of the Jackson's Ridge pub. He'd been the front man for the facility ever since its inception and was a standing testament to the fact that the business operated at a steady loss.

"Hope I didn't disturb your beauty sleep."

Harry shoved a pair of dark glasses on the bridge of his nose and adjusted his hearing aid. "What?"

Dani locked the door of the truck and slung the

strap of her handbag over her shoulder. "I said, new gate I see."

"Uh-huh." He shoved his hands on his hips. "Thinking of opening a café, so folks can have a cup of tea while they buy their ostrich products. Can't let the place go to rack and ruin."

"Why not?" she muttered beneath her breath as she moved into the shade of the veranda.

Harry gave her a blank look. "What?"

"I said it's very hot."

He looked suspicious. "The weather? Yep, it's dry all right."

Dani followed Harry into the cool of the shop. She stared at the shelves stacked with jars of oil and cosmetics and the craft products made from feathers and skin, and repressed a shudder. The thick layer of dust on the lids of the jars told its own story. If Harry had sold one item since she'd last been here a year ago she would eat the sagging leather hat hanging in the corner. To her certain knowledge the only money that flowed into this place came from trapped investors.

Harry led the way into his cramped office, which was situated at one end of the shop, pulled out the chair behind his desk and sat down. "Want to see your bird?"

Dani helped herself to a seat. "Not really."

He cackled, ignoring her. "Sorry, no can do today, the handler's off sick. I'm not supposed to go out to the pens on account of contamination."

Harry's use of the word *handler* made the ostriches sound as dangerous as big cats. "Not a problem. Wouldn't want you to get dirty, Harry."

His brows jerked together. "What? You making a joke about that movie?"

"I said I'll see the bird another day." When hell freezes over to be exact.

She pulled her chequebook from her purse and wrote out the amount owed. It was bad enough having to empty their account on a business venture gone bad—the last thing she wanted was to view the mistake. Harry could keep his ostriches until doomsday if he wanted.

Another vehicle pulled into the car park as she slapped a copy of the contract on the desk. "I want a written receipt for that cheque, and the contract signed off. That's the last payment you get out of Galbraith."

Harry began rummaging in the bottom drawer of the desk, presumably for the receipt book.

Dani was surprised to see Tony Flynn stroll into the office.

He tapped on the door. "Knock, knock. I know you're in there, Harry."

Harry straightened with a grubby book in his hand. "It ain't no secret."

Flynn drew two fingers in a lightning movement. "Bang, bang, you're dead."

Harry froze like a rabbit caught in the headlights, then just as abruptly relaxed. "Very funny. Have you got that cheque for me?"

Flynn blew on the end of his fingers and put his "gun" away. "Unfortunately."

* * *

An hour later, the terminated contract on the kitchen table, Dani celebrated by breaching the "wine cellar"—a cupboard over the kitchen counter which used to be packed with home-made preserves, but these days contained only minimal quantities of Aunt Ellen's experimental fruit wines.

Sitting down at the kitchen table, she eased the cap off a bottle of blackberry nip, sniffed the heady fragrance and poured a small amount into a glass. Ellen's wines might have been experimental, but they were potent.

Halfway through the glass, she tensed at the sound of a footfall. A brief knock on the door and Carter walked into the kitchen. "Looks like you're celebrating."

Dani tilted the glass and sipped. The blackberry nip was so rich and sweet it had practically turned to syrup, but it had ignited a nice glow in her stomach. "I finished with the ostriches today." She frowned as her tongue stumbled on the last word. Absently, she noted that her tongue was beginning to go numb.

Carter eyed the bottle with suspicion. "You did what?"

She tapped the contract, which was sitting on the table. "I paid the final instalment of the ostrich contract."

"I thought you'd done that last year." He helped himself to a chair. "Mind if I join you?"

"Actually, yes."

He studied the bottle of blackberry nip with a jaundiced eye. "I'll get myself a glass."

Dani pushed to her feet. That was Carter in a nutshell, give him an inch and he took a mile. "It's my kitchen, my glass. I'll get it."

The counter seemed a little further away than usual, and a little more difficult to get to. Placing the glass in front of him, she resumed her seat, feeling distinctly on edge.

He poured a syrupy splash of wine. She retrieved the bottle and recorked it, putting an end to the grey area about whether or not either of them should have any more to drink.

"Don't you ever relax?"

"Not lately."

She realized he was checking out the instalment amount, which was visible on the receipt Harry had stapled to the contract.

His gaze connected with hers. "How much money have you got left?"

The base of the glass hit her table with a click. Dani pushed back her chair and rose to her feet. Letting him into her kitchen was borderline; giving him a drink was crazy. "That's none of your business."

The sound of the ticking clock was loud in the kitchen as he studied the contract, making her itch to grab the piece of paper out of his fingers.

"How much?"

She noticed he hadn't so much as sipped the wine. He was stone-cold sober, his control irritating. She walked to the door and opened it. The night air was fresh and cool, making the kitchen seem overheated and stuffy.

"You're broke."

"Not exactly." She had the money from the jewellery to come, and a buyer lined up who wanted to look at the furniture. After she'd sold everything she could possibly stick a price tag on, *then* she would be broke.

With a shrug, Carter moved past her, halting on the veranda.

Dani fixed on the awkwardness in his normally fluid gait. "I didn't know you were missing." The words spilled out, but in that moment she didn't care what they betrayed. He had almost *died*.

"And no one informed you because you're not listed as next of kin. My parents knew—eventually—but they were hamstrung. They were told to keep it quiet."

Dani understood the reasoning, even if she didn't like it. If the press had gotten hold of the story they would have had a field day and jeopardized any chance of rescue. "None of this changes what doesn't work between us."

His gaze sharpened. "Refresh my memory. What exactly is that?"

He was a lot closer than he'd been a second ago. His fingers threaded with hers. If he'd just out-and-out grabbed her, turning him down would have been easy, but the light grip on her fingers bypassed all her defences and he knew it. With a slow, inevitable pressure, he pulled her closer, until she could feel the warmth of his breath on her cheek, and as abruptly as flicking a switch loneliness surged, welling up inside her. As hard as she'd tried not to, she had *missed* him.

His gaze settled on her mouth. "I didn't kiss you last night—and I had the chance."

Her fingers curled into the lapel of his shirt. She could feel the ground dissolving from beneath her feet. "Not fair. You're taking advantage."

His hands settled at her waist. "It's the only advantage I've had in a year."

Her mouth twitched. "Or are likely to get."

His forehead touched against hers. "I called before I shipped out, and a couple of times from Brunei. Some of the calls were picked up, some weren't. The woman who answered didn't explain who she was or that Ellen was ill."

That would have been Harriet. She was gruff and no-nonsense, and as protective as a lioness with cubs. With Ellen critical in hospital, she had volunteered to fend off the constant stream of calls inquiring about Ellen's condition so Dani could get some sleep between hospital visits. At the time, Dani had been in a state of shock and completely absorbed with Ellen. When Ellen had died things had gotten even more disjointed. David, who had been home for the holidays, had taken over, and various neighbours had helped with the arrangements and more or less taken over the phone. "Harriet was here for a couple of weeks."

"Whoever it was, she was like a guard dog."

His mouth came down, shutting off the confused

tangle in her mind and for long minutes she floated
in a sea of pure sensation. Her hands slid up around
his neck as she gave in to the pressure to move in
closer, fitting her body to his and for a few seconds
glorying in the simple animal pleasure of being held.
It had been almost a year since she'd been this close
to Carter, a year since she'd felt female and wanted.

A low humming sound vibrated from his throat,
and abruptly the kiss turned hungry.

A corresponding hunger surged, and with it a
warning. This was where their relationship had always foundered. She always gave ground too fast
and too easy.

Long seconds passed while she forced herself to
catalogue the myriad sensations and somehow find
some distance. Her body felt hot and achy, her skin
ultra sensitive. Kissing Carter wasn't just like stepping close to a fire, it was the equivalent of throw-
ing herself into a blast furnace. Her hands flattened
against his chest. With an effort of will she dragged
oxygen into her lungs and pushed free.

He lifted his head. Inconsequentially, Dani noticed that if she had for one moment thought Carter
was overcome by passion, she would have been
wrong. Aroused he might be, but he was definitely
controlled.

His jaw tightened. "I had a discussion with Wells
today. I can help you through this."

Dani detached herself with difficulty, despite the
fact he was holding her steady more than holding
her. For a moment she had trouble grasping the fact

that he'd been talking to the bank manager. Wells, despite his *GQ* appearance, was the original stuffed shirt. He'd refused to talk about Tom Stoddard's situation with her, but he'd talked about her finances with Carter. The only reason he would have done that was if Carter had linked himself with her relationship-wise.

Stone-cold sober now, she stepped back, using the jamb of the kitchen door for support. "What are you suggesting, exactly?"

His gaze didn't flicker. "Let me help with the money."

"In exchange for what?"

"No strings."

Dani didn't believe him. She studied the line of his jaw, the steady way he watched her. Since he'd come back Carter had changed. He was harder, more abrupt. The physical passion was still there—his drive to get her back in his bed—but there was a coldness underlying it, something almost clinical. She'd turned down his proposition a year ago, now she was certain he was using her financial difficulties as leverage. She knew he was attracted to her and that, like her, he didn't like the vulnerability that came with it. She understood that he wanted to contain and control the relationship in any way he could, but that didn't mean she had to like it.

Galbraith Station was valuable, but it wasn't worth that much, and she figured she was worth a whole lot more.

Her fingers curled around the edge of the door.

With a jerky movement she stepped inside and heaved it closed. "Get lost."

She was in love with Carter—it had happened, period. The extremity of what she felt was singular and terrifying, but she didn't trust it. It made her vulnerable in a way she had never wanted to be.

When Carter reached his kitchen, he picked up the phone and placed a call.

Since quitting the SAS to repair his marriage, Gabriel West had made the transition into the world of commerce as naturally as he'd slipped from his tough street-kid background into undercover operations. What he didn't know about the personalities behind big business in New Zealand wasn't worth knowing.

Carter noted the name of the company that owned the ostrich facility on the notepad beside the phone. When West picked up, Carter was brief and to the point. "I need a favour."

Chapter 9

Dora McIntosh was a monthly appointment and a home visit. An octogenarian and semi-disabled, all Dani could do for her was massage for pain relief and loosen up stiff joints, but they'd both gotten to enjoy the sessions and the afternoon tea that followed. Dora might be slow on her feet, but she was dynamite in the kitchen. People came for miles to visit and eat her scones and plum jam.

Minutes after the physiotherapy session was finished, while Dora was pouring tea into translucent porcelain cups, Dani tensed. She could smell smoke.

Making the excuse that she needed to use the bathroom, just in case she *was* going crazy, she walked down the narrow hallway with its muted runner and faded sepia photographs grouped on the walls. When she opened the door to one of Dora's tiny back bedrooms, smoke and heat blasted out in a wave, sending her stumbling back.

Slamming the door closed, Dani retreated down the hallway, which was now filled with smoke. Dora met her at the kitchen doorway, face pale, eyes frightened. The first order of business was to get Dora to safety. Besides suffering from arthritis, she was an asthmatic; the last thing she needed was an attack brought on by stress or a case of smoke inhalation.

After gathering Dora's handbag and her own things, she turned the knob on the front door. It wouldn't budge. Seconds later, she found that the back door was also locked, and, like the kitchen door, the key was gone.

After a frantic search that came up blank because the entire container of keys was missing, Dani pushed up one of the old-fashioned sash windows, helped Dora out, tossed out their bags and went back for Dora's oxygen.

When she'd made Dora comfortable in the passenger seat of her truck, Dani stood in the dense shade of the walnut tree that overhung the driveway, slipped her cell phone from her bag and made the call. Flames had already engulfed the back third of the house. Dani would do what she could with the garden hose, but Dora lived a good fifteen minutes out of town. By the time the fire crew arrived, it could be too late.

The emergency operator picked up the call and

began taking details. She paused in her list of questions, the tension almost palpable. "Didn't I take a call from you last week?"

The Barclay fire. "That was me. Same person, same town, same kind of emergency, although this time we also need an ambulance."

Less than twenty minutes later, the fire engine came to a halt in front of the house. It was followed by the ambulance and a police cruiser.

Tony Flynn slid through the small knot of medics and fire fighters around the ambulance, the inevitable notepad and pen in his hand. "Who do you think set this fire, Mrs. McIntyre?"

Dora paused as she was being helped into the back of the ambulance. Her gaze settled on the burnt remnants of her cottage. "What makes you think I know anything?"

"Heard Dani Marlow called it in. Again."

The ambulance officer shot Flynn a hard look, and tried to get Dora up the steps.

Dora resisted. "I would have called emergency services myself, but Dani was quicker. If she hadn't been here, I would have died."

"Rumour is if she hadn't been in your house, you'd still have one."

Dora's mouth set in a line. "I don't listen to gossip. Not spoken *or* printed."

The ambulance officer changed his grip, stepping around Dora as he did so and incidentally shouldering Flynn out of the way.

The doors slammed on the ambulance. Seconds

later it was on its way down the drive. Flynn's gaze settled on Dani.

Dani crossed her arms over her chest. "Don't bother."

Flynn's expression lost some of its professional blankness and Dani realized he was loving this. Homes and livelihoods were being destroyed, but for Flynn it was a professional windfall. Career-wise, the Jackson's Ridge fires were the best thing that had happened to him since he'd hit town.

"People are saying whenever you turn up so do the flames."

A shadow fell over Flynn. "If you're trying to snatch a quote out of the air, Flynn, forget it."

Carter. She'd been aware of him in the background, talking to Murdoch and Jackson's Ridge's only other police officer, Lowell Higgins. He must have arrived within seconds of the police cruiser. The only way that could have happened was if Murdoch had phoned him.

Flynn flipped his notebook closed and slipped it into his shirt pocket. "Just doing my job, Rawlings."

"First time I heard fiction was a legal part of it."

Flynn's face hardened. "What exactly are you accusing me of?"

"Nothing. Yet."

Flynn barely registered the threat. Transferring his attention to Dani, he slipped a business card out of his pocket. "If you want to talk I can get you a deal on syndication, maybe even a chunk of dough from a magazine. Think about it."

Dani ignored the card. "Keep it, I won't be changing my mind." In Dani's opinion, even if she had something to say, Flynn had brought a style of reporting to Jackson's Ridge that the small community just didn't need. The general consensus was that he was a city boy, as hard as nails and brash, but he would adjust to the slower, gentler pace in time. So far, despite Flynn's enthusiasm for owning his own paper, he hadn't shown any visible signs of softening, all he'd done was get up everyone's nose.

A loud crumping sound was followed by an explosion of smoke and steam as the roof on Dora's cottage collapsed inward. Walter Douglas roared an order and the men directing a steady stream of water into the building pulled back as a wall collapsed outward.

A slow burning anger ignited as Dani watched walls fall like dominoes. Within a matter of minutes Dora's home—the house she'd lived in for sixty years—had been reduced to little more than a pile of smoking rubble, the pretty gardens around it destroyed. The fact that Flynn, and others, thought she might be responsible for the destruction faded in the face of what Dora had lost.

A chill slid down her spine when she remembered the locked doors. In the scramble to get Dora to safety the cold deliberation of the act—locking them in the house while the fire was set—had barely registered. She'd simply opened a window and kept moving, but now that she had time to think, the intent behind the act took on a distinctly sinister note. Dora didn't normally lock her doors, nor did she leave the keys sitting in the locks. Like everything else in Dora's house they were kept with meticulous order—in a pottery bowl on the kitchen counter. The entire bowl had been missing, which meant that part of the crime had been as premeditated as the carefully set fire in the back bedroom—the room furthest away from the main living rooms of the house—where the blaze could get a good hold before they realised there was a problem.

This fire hadn't been lit by kids or a straight-out pyromaniac, it was the work of an ordered adult mind. She was certain the fire had been set with the intent to panic and injure, maybe even to kill. *She* wasn't an arsonist—or a potential murderer—but someone else was. The problem would be convincing Murdoch of that fact.

On cue, Pete Murdoch pushed through the knot of locals that had arrived to help. He nodded at Carter who had taken up a position beside her and for once Dani didn't have one qualm about Carter's presence or the subtext that went with it. Something had happened since her revelation of the previous day—the resistance that had always existed was gone. The issues that had destroyed their relationship remained and she didn't know if she would ever be comfortable with the vulnerability that went with being in love, but on a subtle female level she had accepted him. She didn't know how they would work things out, or if they ever could, but she didn't question his right to protect her.

After initial pleasantries, Murdoch slid his notebook out of his pocket, but when Flynn appeared, he rolled his eyes and jerked his head in the direction of his cruiser.

Grimly, Dani fell in step beside Carter, and suspicion coalesced into certainty. "Murdoch's the reason you're here."

"He rang me when he got the call. We've got a theory."

"I hope it matches mine."

Dani perched on the edge of the front passenger seat and answered the standard questions. When Murdoch was finished she pushed to her feet. "Ever think that whoever's setting these fires is doing it to frame me?"

Murdoch snapped his notebook closed. "Or using you as a scapegoat. I've put some thought into it."

Carter straightened from his position against the bonnet of the cruiser. "So far almost every fire has been a neighbour."

Murdoch looked thoughtful. "Or a client."

Dani went still inside. The moment she'd discovered Dora's keys were missing replayed itself. She'd assumed the crime was aimed at harming Dora, but if Dora had a connection to the arsonist, it was a random one. Dani's connection was direct in every case: she had been present at every fire. If the link forged by the arsonist was planned and not a coincidence, that could mean she had been the target, not Dora. *"My appointment book."*

She was a creature of habit; her life usually ran like clockwork with little variation. The thought that someone was using that information when committing the crimes in order to implicate her didn't make sense, but it was possible. Briefly, she explained about the keys and the locked doors.

Murdoch made a note. "How accessible is your office?"

"When I'm not there it's locked." Unlike the house, she always secured the clinic. The habit wasn't logical in light of the fact that every other building was wide open, but the precaution was ingrained because she stored confidential medical records. It was second nature to lock up her workspace.

Carter's expression was grim. "The doors may be secured, but the locks are old-fashioned and standard. You can buy the keys from almost any hardware store."

"If a key was needed at all." Most appointments were made at least a couple of weeks in advance, so the book was filled. All it would take was a glance from someone in her waiting room. "The theory has holes. Tom's a client, but not on a regular basis, and I've never treated Nola."

Murdoch shrugged. "At this point, any lead works for me."

The now-familiar figure of O'Halloran standing watching the fire crew roll up hose registered. "O'Halloran was in for a treatment last week."

Murdoch's gaze was cold. "Don't worry, I'm checking on him."

* * *

Half an hour later, Murdoch was in Dani's therapy rooms, studying her client list and the appointment book. "Mind if I borrow these? I'll copy it and have it back to you tomorrow."

Dani took a note of the week's appointments then dug out her address book. "You might want this, too."

Murdoch shook his head. "I had no idea you treated so many people out here." His expression was unreadable as he bagged the books and placed them in his briefcase.

Her stomach tightened at the possibility that one of her clients was responsible for the fires, and for setting her up.

Murdoch straightened. "Made any enemies lately?"

"None that I can think of." Jackson's Ridge had always been a haven. People *liked* her, and she liked them.

But, chances were, someone on that list didn't, and it wasn't comforting to know that over the last month she had been busier than ever with the practice.

Dani watched as Murdoch drove away.

Carter pushed a hot drink into her hands.

"He's still going to investigate me."

Carter propped himself against the doorjamb and sipped his coffee. "It's his job."

The brevity of his reply and his rock-solid steadiness were oddly comforting.

"I notice Walter was on that list."

Dani wrapped her fingers around the mug and breathed in the fragrance of the coffee. "Walter's been coming to me for years. It's no big deal. Chronic sciatica."

Carter finished his drink in silence, straightened and walked to the small kitchenette.

She heard water running as he rinsed his mug. "It *can't* be Walter."

Carter reappeared. "He's been in the Fire Service for years."

Dani didn't need a picture drawn. She'd watched the movies and read the newspaper articles. Criminals loved to revisit the scene of the crime, and firebugs got their thrills by watching the fire. What better way to observe than if you were actually on the fire crew? She shook her head. "It can't be Walter."

"Someone's setting the fires. They're skilled and elusive, and you're at the centre of the pattern."

The clear, cold blue of Carter's gaze was unsettling. The word *pattern* didn't make her feel any better.

She lifted the mug to her mouth and drank, forcing herself to shake off the jumpy feeling. "What do you know about patterns?"

"It's part of what I do."

The reply didn't do a thing to settle her nerves. Dani had studied the SAS as much as a civilian and an outsider could, but the information available in books and documentaries only provided a glimpse of the world he moved in. "What *exactly* is it that you do?"

When he answered his voice was flat, his face expressionless. Some of his missions were peace-keeping ones, and some weren't, because primarily he was an assault specialist. He wasn't going to give her any specific details, because no one needed to know that much, but a lot of his work was undercover. His last mission, a peacekeeping detail in a relatively stable area, should have been a walk in the park—instead it had almost killed him. The one before that had been high-risk and co-vert. He had been inserted into a foreign country to hunt a terrorist. It had taken months, but he had found him.

The idea of Carter systematically hunting down a terrorist made her blood run cold. The fact that he had run the man to ground in home territory made the chill deepen. She had always been aware of Carter's physical and mental competence—it per-meated everything he did. Now she realized that the surface charm was almost a complete blind. It had fooled a lot of people, and it had fooled her. For years she'd been so busy coping with the persona he projected that she'd missed the real man be-neath.

Her heart pounded and her chest felt constricted. "What are you going to do?" Because it was a cer-tainty that Carter had something planned.

He stared at the sere brown hills and the benign glimpse of sea visible between trees. "Hunt him."

Chapter 10

An hour later, showered and dressed, Carter stepped out on his veranda and studied the vehicles parked at Dani's clinic.

Murdoch had his theories, and he had his, but their approaches were distinctly different. Murdoch was concerned with evidence and motivation—the lawful apprehension of the perpetrator. Carter just wanted to nail the guy.

Strolling back inside, he grabbed a pair of high-resolution binoculars then headed down to the beach road.

A few minutes later, he went down on his haunches to study the road surface where it petered out into a large, flat area of grass and scrub. If anyone had parked a vehicle down here recently, he should be able to find some trace.

Rising to his feet, he circled the open area and discovered a set of tracks that disappeared behind a thick patch of manuka. He followed the tracks and found a flattened area beneath the shady overhang of one of the gnarled pohutukawa trees that dotted the edge of the bush line. From the depth of the tire indentations, and the trampled area, it had been used several times. It was possible that whoever had parked here had just come for the fishing, but not likely. Having to carry fishing gear and bait through the scrub would be a major pain, and there was plenty of secluded parking closer to the beach.

Reaching into his pocket he extracted his cell phone and put through a call to Murdoch.

Gabriel West stared at the view of the sea from Carter's kitchen. "Nice spot to settle down."

"Don't start."

West stared critically at Carter's leg. "Wound's healed up nicely, but you're still stiff. You should think about getting yourself some physio."

Carter filled the kettle at the sink and plugged it in. "I've tried to get an appointment. She can't fit me in."

"She?"

Carter jerked his head toward Dani's place.

West studied the graceful colonial lines of the adjacent house as Carter made tea, and caught a glimpse of red hair as a tall, lean woman walked from the house to a set of outbuildings and disappeared from view. Suddenly a lot of things about

Carter began to make sense. The reason his hometown and the farm had become so important over the last couple of years, for example. "Your next-door neighbour, huh?"

"You make that sound significant."

"It depends. How long has she been your neighbour?"

"Forever."

West gave Carter a look that could have been termed inscrutable if Carter didn't know what was going on behind the bland facade. West had a sixth sense when it came to combat situations, and an uncanny luck—until he'd gotten shot *after* he'd left the SAS. He also had a quiet knack for getting to the truth of things in civilian life…eventually.

Carter set steaming mugs in front of West and his wife, Tyler, grabbed the sugar bowl on the way back to the table, hooked out a chair with his foot and sat down. He didn't miss the speculative silence. Slow seconds ticked by while he stirred sugar into his tea. When he lifted his head, West was once again examining the view. Resigned, Carter set his mug down. "*And?*"

West's expression didn't change. "And what?"

Carter's jaw tightened, a nerve in his cheek began to twitch. Ever since he'd gotten home, he'd had to keep a tight rein on his temper; right now, on a scale of one to ten he was at about eight and he was deteriorating fast. As far as he was concerned, talking about relationship problems was about as pleasurable as pulling teeth. It was also a known fact that

West as a confidant was close to useless. On the other hand Dani *had* been his neighbour for eighteen years and he'd been dangling on a string for just about that long. He shrugged. "Any suggestions?"

"Nope."

Carter let out a breath.

Tyler lifted an eyebrow. "What did you expect? If he's a love doctor then so is the sphinx."

The silence that followed Tyler's statement was profound. Carter kept his expression carefully blank as he settled back in his chair. Time for a change of subject. West's lack of relationship skills had always been a sore point with Tyler. The couple were happy now, but it had taken West eight years to admit he had a problem with emotion, let alone make a start on patching up his marriage. Carter eyed West's briefcase. "So, what *have* you got for me?"

"A whole lot I didn't expect to find." West flipped the locks and pulled out a sheet of paper. He slid the page across to Carter. "Do those names mean anything to you?"

Amongst the list, Carter recognized the name of a prominent New Zealand businessman, Alex Bainbridge—a big hitter on the local stock market—and the name of a local farmer, Dave, who managed a large station on the other side of town. A third name, Jordan Carlisle, tantalized.

West sat back in his chair. "It's a complicated trail, but I eventually found the links. Bainbridge is a director of Jackson's Bay Holdings—the company that owns the large station McLean manages. Jackson's Bay Holdings, through a subsidiary company, is also the major shareholder in the ostrich facility. Carlisle is a financier who's been tied up with Bainbridge for years. The ostrich farm itself is a lemon— and the largest beneficiary of the losses are Bainbridge and Carlisle. In fact I wouldn't be surprised to learn that they own the other company that has a small holding in it, because the facility is operated purely as a taxable write-off—not nice, but legitimate. The interesting thing is that the ostrich facility is on a prime piece of real estate—close to the beach and the town. I pulled a few strings and got a look at the syndicate's first-stage development plans for the Jackson's Bay resort. The main resort buildings are sited on the land presently occupied by the ostrich facility. To complicate matters, Bainbridge is on the board of directors of the bank the syndicate are using to finance their development. As it happens, that's Jackson's Ridge's only bank."

Carter sat back in his chair. He was beginning to feel happier. "And they've been folding on mortgages."

"You've got it." West slotted the pages in his suitcase with the same casual precision Carter knew he would use to bury Bainbridge and Carlisle and possibly Wells. "The links I've uncovered are enough to stop the resort project."

"On another level entirely." Carter pulled a device that looked like a remote control from his pocket and placed it on the table. He pressed a button; the liquid-crystal screen glowed. "I borrowed it from the local vet. It's a microchip scanner. A lot of pedigree dog owners are using them, but apparently that's also how you identify your bird, by the number encoded into the microchip embedded in its neck."

West set his mug down. "Should be interesting."

West held the rear passenger door of Carter's truck open for Tyler and the dog that had adopted them—a lean streak of huntaway called Zoom. Zoom settled in beside Tyler, head erect, gaze focused on the windscreen, almost more human than dog. As West closed the door, he caught another glimpse of red hair and long tanned legs through the trees that separated the Galbraith and Rawlings houses. "How long did you say you've been living next door to Dani?"

"Like I said, forever. Eighteen years."

West shook his head. "And you gave me a hard time."

Dani slid into the driver's seat of the truck and turned the key in the ignition. The motor turned over then died. Muttering a brief prayer, she held her breath, pumped the accelerator and turned the key again. This time the only sound was a click.

Gritting her teeth, she slid out of the driver's seat. Like the tractor, she'd been babying the truck for weeks. It was due for a service and its six-monthly warrant of fitness. She could do without the service, because she'd changed the oil and the filters herself, but at present it was in no state to pass the warrant.

One of the rear brake lights was gone and two of the tires were close to bald, although in this case neither of those things was the problem. The dead little click indicated the battery had probably died.

She searched for the catch of the bonnet and heaved upward. "If it turns out to be the starter motor, I'll probably shoot the truck."

"I'll lend you the gun," Carter murmured. "It should have been put down years ago."

Dani almost dropped the bonnet as Carter walked out of bright sunshine into the dimness of the garage. "Careful. In vehicle terms this is close to antique. It could be worth a lot of money."

"In an alternate universe where baling twine and rust mean something, maybe…"

Latching the bonnet, Dani picked up a screwdriver and began chiselling a thick layer of bluish crystals off the battery terminals.

"If you pour boiling water over the oxide it'll take it right off."

Dani let out a breath and counted and tried not to notice Carter looking certifiably gorgeous in a dazzling white T-shirt and butt-hugging jeans. "What do you want, Carter? As you can see, I'm busy."

"Then it's time you had an afternoon off. Want to go and see your new bird?"

"Not really." Pulling fingernails out would be a more pleasurable pastime.

She was acutely aware of him watching her as she continued to work at the terminals.

"How old is that battery?"

Setting the screwdriver down on the bench, she grabbed a rag, wiped her hands, then dropped the bonnet. "Five years. I'm in denial." She'd already done the calculation and figured it was ready for the scrap heap. Leaning in the driver's-side door, she tried the key. The dead click confirmed what she already knew.

"Either way, you're going to need a ride into town."

"You could offer to pick up a battery for me."

"Trust me, you need to check out the bird.".

"I know what they look like." And how much they cost.

With a shrug, Carter slid a pair of dark glasses on the bridge of his nose and strolled toward his truck, which was parked beneath a shady tree.

Reluctantly, Dani slid the key out of the ignition and followed him. Ostriches or not, Carter was right, she needed that battery.

One of the rear windows of Carter's truck slid down as she approached. A glossy strand of tawny hair shivered in the breeze and Dani's stomach tightened. For the second time in two days there was a woman in his truck—and this one was pregnant.

Carter's gaze connected with hers, and she wondered if he'd read her mind. "They're a couple of friends from Auckland. Gabe and Tyler West."

Dani registered the dark-haired man sitting next to Tyler as she gripped the handle of the passenger-side door. She'd heard Carter talk about the Wests, she'd even seen their wedding portrait in Carter's lounge, but this was the first time Carter had ever introduced her to any of his SAS friends.

As she fastened her seat belt, a dog's narrow head popped over one shoulder and the woman's inquisitive stare in the rear view mirror immediately gave way to a bright smile. "Hi, I'm Tyler, and this is Zoom. You must be Dani. Carter's told me all about you."

Dani forced a smile and made a polite rejoinder. "Are you staying?"

"Only until Gabe can book a motel." She patted her stomach. "We don't want to be too far out from town with this little guy on the way."

Several vehicles were parked at the ostrich facility. Dani was surprised to recognize Walter Douglas's truck slotted beside Roger Wells's gleaming new car, which now had a bank slogan emblazoned on the side.

West helped Tyler out. His gaze fixed on the glimpse of beach between a straggly line of windblown trees. "Million-dollar view."

Carter climbed out from behind the wheel. "Not exactly prime ostrich country."

Dani snapped her door closed. "What is?"

A sporty hatchback pulled into the car park, slotting next to Carter's truck. Tony Flynn's thin smile flashed as he climbed out. "What a surprise."

Dani eyed the camera hung around his neck. "Only if you weren't following us." She'd noticed his vehicle just seconds after they'd pulled out onto the county road. Flynn was a lot of things, but he wasn't subtle.

"It's not against the law to drive on the open road."

Carter locked the truck and pocketed the keys. "It might be if harassment's involved."

Flynn's expression didn't change. "Now I'm scared."

Harry strolled out onto the shaded porch and shoved on a pair of dark glasses. He peered at Flynn. "What are you doin' back here?"

"Came to buy some ostrich oil. For my gun. You got any?"

"What?" Harry twiddled with his ear.

Dani strode past Flynn. Now that she was here, she just wanted to get the viewing over and done with. "He can't hear you, his hearing aid's not turned up."

Harry's head swivelled in her direction. "You don't have to yell." He glared at Flynn. "What do you want—you've paid."

"Don't remind me. What's Wells doing here?" Flynn's expression grew hopeful. "This place going broke?"

"Smart, huh? Better watch your mouth."

"Or what? You gonna blow me away?"

"Huh?" He peered at Flynn. His head swivelled, his gaze fixed on Dani. "You want to see your bird?"

"Offhand I can't think of any other reason to be here."

"You'll have to wait. Walter's just viewing his bird."

Carter stepped up onto the veranda, dwarfing Harry. "What's the wait for?"

"You gotta wait on Jim. He's the only one who can deal with the birds." Harry shook his head. "Damn dangerous." He turned on his heel then stopped. He gestured at the lone plastic table with two chairs that was set up on the veranda. "If you want a cup of tea we've got a café here, just take a seat."

Tyler studied the grimy surface of the table. "I wonder who the waitress is?"

Harry stamped inside. He disappeared from view then appeared in his office window, an electric kettle in his hand.

Carter slipped off his dark glasses and stepped inside. "Guess that answers that question."

Harry made a production of opening the gate.

Walter Douglas was leaning on the fence, in conversation with Roger Wells. Jim was in the far corner of the pen, armed with a broom: he had an ostrich cornered. Jim aimed a scanner at the bird. "This one's yer bird, Walter."

Walter stared at the big bird with its long neck and beady eyes. "Great," he said glumly.

Jim turned his back on the bird. A small head snaked down, Jim made a gargling sound. The bird ducked, avoiding Jim's clumsy fend with the broom and strutted back to join the motley group of birds clustered in the opposite corner of the pen.

Harry's gaze fixed on the birds with a kind of horrified fascination, giving credence to the blunt statement he'd made shortly after the facility had opened, that he "wasn't never goin' near those birds." He cleared his throat. "Another customer for you, Jim."

"Client," Jim snapped.

Harry didn't take his gaze off the birds. "Whatever."

Carter leaned on the fence and gave Jim what Dani termed the standard "guy" look. "Looks like you run a tight operation."

Jim's expression took on a defensive cast. "I just show people their birds."

"Be interested to know how many you've got."

"Enough. Couldn't tell you offhand." Jim's expression grew hopeful. "Not unless you wanted to invest?"

Carter's eyes glazed over. "Let's not worry about numbers today."

Dani stared at the ostriches. They looked like they were a long way from home. Every time she saw the birds she experienced the same sense of disbelief. With the struggle and challenge of sheep and cattle farming she couldn't understand why anyone would want to buy into something so exotic and risky. As far as she was concerned, if she could meet her mortgage payments, that was enough excitement to last her for the next ten years.

Jim marched toward the cluster of birds. They flowed around him then reformed in the adjacent corner. Face reddened with exertion, he finally managed to separate the birds into two groups. Seconds later, he cornered an ostrich.

"Looks like a random choice," Carter murmured. "I thought he was going for the big one."

"The big one?" Dani stared at the remaining birds, which had reformed into a single group. "From here they all look big."

"It's not a random choice." As Jim pulled his scanner out of his pocket, Carter opened the tall metal gate and walked into the enclosure.

"Hey you can't come in here—"

Carter's gaze fixed on the ostrich. "Is that Dani's bird?"

"Of course it's her—"

"Have you checked?"

"I don't need to. I reared these birds from chicks. What I don't know about them isn't worth knowing."

Carter slipped the scanner he'd borrowed from his pocket and stepped closer to the bird.

Jim's face took on a purple tinge. "Hey! What are you doing?"

"Same as you. Checking." He studied the reading then compared it with the one still showing on Jim's scanner. "This is the same bird you just said belonged to Walter."

The conversation between Wells and Walter stopped.

Carter slipped a document from his pocket. Dani's gaze sharpened as he unfolded the sheets. It looked suspiciously like her ostrich contract. She hadn't been aware it was missing but, after the kiss on her veranda the other night, keeping track of that particular piece of paperwork hadn't exactly been a priority. The last time she could remember seeing it was when Carter had been studying the amount noted on the receipt, after that, things had gotten a little confused.

But if things had been hazy for Dani, they hadn't been for Carter. She had known the kiss had been a deliberate tester. He had wanted to gauge his progress, and he had wanted to soften her up before he'd made his offer of financial help. He hadn't achieved everything he had wanted, she hadn't allowed him to tie her to him financially, but he had stepped in closer to her, putting their relationship back on a physical footing—and he had obtained information he had wanted.

Carter had a ruthless streak—she had always known it. He'd made no secret about the fact that he wanted her back or that, as he'd stated a year ago, he wanted to tie her to him—on his terms.

She didn't trust him, period. If ever she'd needed a reminder of exactly what it was that made her wary, this was it.

Grimly, she watched as he ran the device down the ostrich's neck and checked the number registering on the screen with the number noted on the contract. "Looks like I owe you an apology. This *is* Dani's bird."

Jim blinked, the broom wavered.

He continued to scan down the bird's neck. "And Walter's and about...six others'." With a deft movement, he slipped the contract back in his shirt pocket and took the broom off Jim, releasing the stressed bird. "Besides fraud there's got to be a law against inserting eight microchips in an animal's neck."

Wells looked interested. "What is that device?"

Carter slipped the scanner back in his pocket. "A microchip scanner, the same thing Jim's using. It picks up the individual codes. The ostrich facility has just over one hundred investors. From what I've seen there are only about thirty birds. Would that be right, Jim?"

A vein at Jim's temple pulsed. "I'm just the handler, Harry does the figures."

Harry's eyes bugged.

Walter went bright red. "I just wrote out a cheque."

Carter didn't take his attention off Jim. "If I were you, Walter, I'd go and get it."

Walter's head jerked in assent. "Right."

Jim took a step forward. "Hey you can't do—"

Carter blocked him. "What? Get back the money you just stole from him?"

Harry's expression took on an indignant cast. "We ain't stole nothing."

West straightened from his relaxed position against the fence. "Who's your boss?"

A vein throbbed at Jim's temple. "Don't say a word, Harry. Not until he comes up with a warrant."

"There's a thought." Carter pulled out his cell phone and put through a call. "Murdoch's going to love this."

Jim went pale.

West pulled a slip of paper out of his pocket. "Ever heard of Alex Bainbridge?"

Harry blinked, Jim kept his gaze on the ostriches.

"He owns Jackson's Bay Holdings, which makes him your boss. He also runs the syndicate that's been buying up farms and businesses."

A nervous tic started on the side of Jim's jaw.

Dani frowned, a flicker of movement distracting her. Flynn was visible in Harry's office, and it looked as if he was searching it. "Jackson's Bay Holdings. That's John McLean. Didn't he marry a Bainbridge? Hetty Bainbridge."

Carter slipped his cell phone in his pocket and strolled back to the fence, his limp barely perceptible. "McLean's *wife* is a Bainbridge?"

Dani shrugged. "Aunt Ellen had a friend in Mason who went to school with her. Not many people know it, but Hetty McLean is Alex Bainbridge's half-sister."

The metal gate clanged behind Carter. "That's it, he's sunk."

West shook his head. "Small towns. You gotta love 'em."

"Did I hear you say Bainbridge?"

Dani turned to find Wells right behind her. "That's right. We're just discussing the coincidence that Alex Bainbridge's name seems to be all over the place lately."

Jim's expression grew panicked. "Can't see how. The first time I've heard it is today."

Dani lifted a brow. The nervous tic on Jim's jaw had gone crazy, which probably meant he was lying through his teeth. "Then you better get used to it."

She jerked her head toward Harry's office, where Flynn's shadowy figure was still visible. "Once Flynn gets hold of the story, no one's going to be talking about anything else for a month."

Wells looked increasingly uncomfortable. "I think we need to talk. In private."

Chapter 11

In the moonlight the chain-link fences of the ostrich facility glinted a ghostly silver. A faint breeze blew in off the sea, stirring the humid air and rustling through the tough leaves of the stunted manuka trees and short, bristly coprosma bushes that bordered the beach.

A truck, its headlights doused, idled past the facility and ghosted to a halt. Seconds later, a man exited the vehicle, collected a knapsack from the passenger seat and moved on foot toward the facility.

The wind lifted as he walked, making the sign above the gates creak. When he reached the gates, he shrugged out of the knapsack, extracted a pair of heavy-duty bolt cutters and snipped through the chain that fastened the gates.

Slipping the bolt cutters back into the knapsack, he stepped through the opening.

Grinning coldly, he walked the perimeter and cut jagged holes in the chain-link fences. When he was finished, he examined his handiwork with a critical eye.

The facility had more than served its purpose.

Carter removed his night-vision goggles and examined the pale line of surf, faintly luminescent and easily visible now that the moon was up. Systematically, he skimmed the dark folds of the hills that plunged down to the beach, waiting for his vision to adjust.

Shifting position, he eased the stiffness out of his leg. As on the last three nights, the beach and the hills were empty. Whoever had been concealing their vehicle in the scrub and prowling around Dani's place hadn't been back.

Minutes ticked by. A subtle change in the air made him tense. A warm gust of wind intensified the faint drift, turning it acrid. Smoke. Simultaneously, a shift in the shadows caught his attention. He tracked the movement as a dark shape glided from tree to tree until he could identify the outline. The figure was male, tall and well-built.

Keeping his gaze fixed on the figure, Carter began to climb, gauging the point at which his path would intersect with the intruder's—at the edge of the smooth sweep of lawn just below Dani's house.

Minutes later, bracing himself against the stiffening pain in his thigh, he surged forward, grabbed the man's wrist and took him down to the ground in one fluid movement. A knee jabbed into his belly as the man rolled, elusive as a snake. Something metallic skittered across the dusty ground and the intruder lunged, wrenching free of Carter's hold with a neat twist. Carter caught him by one leg then reared back as a boot caught him in the jaw. Ears ringing, he countered with a wrestling move, lunging forward and using his weight to shove sideways, pinning the intruder on his back.

Moonlight slanted across the man's face.

"O'Halloran."

Detective O'Halloran to be precise. A former member of the Special Tactics Squad. Carter hadn't ever met him personally, but he knew a couple of ex-SAS guys in the squad who had worked with him. Eighteen months previously O'Halloran had headed up an arson investigation. In the process his own home had been targeted and burned down, with his wife and child in it. O'Halloran had tried to save them and failed, ending up in hospital.

Gaze cold, a second, more elusive shadow watched Rawlings and O'Halloran converse from the deep well of shade cast by a towering oak. He couldn't make out what they were saying, but their topic of conversation wasn't in doubt. Silently, he retreated further back into the deep cover of the trees hemming the Galbraith house, glad that he'd listened to his instincts and used an alternative route.

When he was sure the coast was clear, he slipped further back into the shadows, skirting the moonlight-drenched stretches of lawn as he made his way to the barn.

In the distance a familiar siren sounded.

Finally someone had noticed that the ostrich facility was burning.

The siren jerked Murdoch out of sleep, seconds later his pager, which was stationed on the bedside table, began to vibrate. Pushing the covers back, he checked the message, climbed out of bed and searched out a fresh uniform. His wife, used to his odd hours, didn't stir. Her hair was soft and rumpled on the pillow, her face smooth. Murdoch envied her the calm oblivion. Lately, the sound of the siren was beginning to haunt him.

Ten minutes later, after he'd put a call through to the two Mason detectives who'd been assigned to Jackson's Ridge as backup for the fires, he picked Lowell up and headed out to the ostrich facility.

A kilometre out, something large darted off the road. Murdoch swerved; his headlights caught a flash of white and the gangling outline of an ostrich. As he drove, he glimpsed flighty movement along the sides of the road, in the paddocks and even down on the beach, which was visible from the road. There were ostriches everywhere.

Cursing beneath his breath, he brought the cruiser to a halt beside what remained of the facility. Given that both of Jackson's Ridge's ostrich "experts" had spent the evening in town at the pub it was unlikely that either Harry or Jim would be in any state to recover the birds. He'd once read somewhere that those birds could clock up to thirty miles an hour, and counting. By morning they would be in Mason. Someone was going to have to round them up, and fast.

The fire truck was parked just inside the open gates, its lights strobing. According to the information he'd gotten from emergency services, they had responded quickly, but even so the main building was a smoking ruin.

As he climbed from the cruiser a lean figure was briefly visible in the flash of a camera. Flynn had beaten him to the fire and was already busy taking pictures.

Murdoch slammed his door. "Don't you ever sleep, Flynn?"

"I do my job, Murdoch, you do yours."

"So why does mine seem so much more worthwhile?"

Flynn clicked the shutter, the flash lit up the night. He lowered the camera, not bothering to hide his amusement. "It's not a good idea to upset the media."

"Better wipe that smile off your face, I hear you had shares in this place, which puts you on my list of suspects."

Flynn didn't bother to adjust his expression. "In that case, you could be indicting the whole town."

A burly figure in a helmet and coverall appeared out of the gloom, backlit by the dying glow of the fire.

Walter Douglas took off his helmet and wiped his face. "Half a dozen ignition points. Whoever lit this one wanted it to burn. Even lit up some of the fences." He shook his head. "They had containers of ostrich oil in there. That didn't help."

"Heard you got here early—again."

Walter's face grew cautious. "Some evenings I stay late at the station." He turned his gaze back on the smoking ruin. "Now that Lily's gone there isn't an awful lot else to do."

Lily was Walter's wife. Ex-wife now. A couple of years ago she'd moved back to live on her family's orchard. The fact that Lily Douglas, née Barclay, was living at the address of the first fire to hit Jackson's Ridge was something that had been keeping Murdoch awake at night. He liked Walter, he didn't want to find a reason for him to be the arsonist, but when it was staring him in the face it was more than his job was worth to ignore it. "Even so, seems to me you're spending a lot of time hanging out at the fire station."

The pump sputtered and the hose deflated. Walter shoved his helmet back on his head and roared an order. For a few seconds the air turned blue as Walter undid the coupling from the empty water tank and transferred the hose to the second, smaller appliance pulled up beside the main truck, getting drenched in the process. The new pump started, stuttered, then settled into a steady rhythm. Flaccid hose bloated out and embers hissed as the new stream of water hit the last remaining hot spot. Walter, still swearing, wiped water and soot off his face and bellowed instructions.

Murdoch waited out the process as the last hot spots were doused. This was the country. One of the refreshing differences he enjoyed about the place was that people here were blunter and more direct. Of course there were exceptions and, lately, Jackson's Ridge had taken on a whole new feel he didn't like. Families that went way back were leaving town, their properties and beach houses bought up by the syndicate that wanted to turn the place into a resort—the houses left derelict. On top of that farmers were going broke because of the drought—and now these fires.

Taking out his notebook, he flipped it open and turned his attention back to Walter. There was no point in beating about the bush. "Since when have you taken to hanging out at the station at night, Walter?"

Walter's face reddened. "What are you getting at?"

Murdoch transferred his gaze to the fire crew, who were now rolling up hose. "Nothing, except that all that solitude can't be good. You should get out more, maybe get some counselling. A marriage breakup is never easy."

Walter's face was stony. "I don't need counselling. Lily left two years ago. It was tough, but I handled it."

"One more question."

Walter's face reddened. "I'm putting the fire out, I didn't light it."

"You've got shares in this place."

"And I'd be crazy to light it up. Those scamming bastards owe *me* money."

Murdoch scratched his head. That was where the logic on this one fell over. Walter was right. Burning the place now just didn't make sense.

A vehicle pulled up behind his cruiser. Murdoch let out a breath. Rawlings and O'Halloran. Why did he have the feeling that a messy night had just gotten more complicated?

A second vehicle swerved into the water table, parking askew. The driver's door flew open and Harry Tapp lurched onto the road. He stared blearily at the building.

Murdoch blocked Harry's path. "There's been a fire."

Harry gave him a blank look, which meant he'd turned his hearing aid off. "*What?*"

Murdoch took a step back. Harry's breath was one-hundred-percent alcohol. If he got too close to a naked flame, he'd probably ignite. Murdoch tried to blank out the fact that despite being drunk, Harry had *driven* to the fire. Irritating as he was, he'd just lost his livelihood; sometimes you had to turn a blind eye. He pitched his voice just short of a bellow. "We need to ask you a few questions."

Murdoch jerked his head at Lowell.

Lowell frowned when Murdoch explained what he wanted. "What am I supposed to ask?"

Not for the first time Murdoch wondered what it would feel like to take one of the little happy pills a doctor had once prescribed him for stress. At the time he hadn't succumbed to temptation. He'd decided that if he were going to have a breakdown he'd rather have it out of the city, in a quiet country town where no one knew him—and without the medication. "Just keep him busy."

Lowell sidled closer to Harry, then stumbled back. Murdoch grinned, the perverse sense of humour that had kept him sane surfacing. "And Lowell…"

Lowell darted him a blank look.

"Question him about the ostriches."

Carter studied the charred building and all the people present. Murdoch was there along with Lowell and a couple of other cops who were unfamiliar—reinforcements from Mason. Now that the fire was out, crime scene tape was already being strung around what was left of the building.

Murdoch's greeting was accompanied by a hard glance at O'Halloran. "If you want to help, stay off the site and round up those birds. Lowell's got his hands full controlling Harry—" he jerked his thumb at the two city cops "—and those two guys won't move from the scene."

Carter made a call. Minutes later the flash of headlights as a car approached drew his attention.

West exited the car, his gaze settling on O'Halloran. "You're a long way from Auckland Central."

O'Halloran's expression didn't change. "I suppose I shouldn't be surprised to see you here."

West shrugged. "I get around."

"I heard."

The previous year West and Carter had both been involved in the bust of a notorious jewel thief and a gang that fenced artefacts. Carter had escaped publicity, but West hadn't been so lucky. The story and some of his previous exploits had made the front page of both the city paper and a national tabloid. O'Halloran, an inner-city detective, hadn't worked that case— but only because he had been in hospital at the time.

An ostrich jogged past the opened gate, heading for the beach.

O'Halloran studied the bird's gait. "How do you catch those things?"

Lowell looked depressed. "Harry said you get 'em with brooms, but all the brooms burned."

"Looks like it's your lucky day." Carter reached into the rear of his truck and tossed him a broom just as a large horse trailer came to a halt outside the gates.

Lowell caught the broom, then just as promptly dropped it.

"And Lowell?"

Lowell straightened, handling the broom as if it was an automatic weapon without the safety.

Carter's expression was deadpan. "Wait until you see the whites of their eyes."

The ramp dropped on the back of the horse trailer. John McKay led out three horses, all saddled and ready to go. He handed the bridle of a rangy chestnut to Carter. "Don't tell me *you've* got an ostrich contract."

"I didn't have time to sign up."

John swung up onto a tall bay. "Then you must be the only one."

Carter jerked his head, indicating West could take the remaining horse.

West backed off. "I am *not* getting up on one of those things." Back streets and alleys were his environment, not the Wild West. "O'Halloran, it's all yours."

With a shrug, O'Halloran swung into the saddle, wincing at the stiffness in his neck and shoulder. He'd had a farm background before he was a cop, in theory he could do this.

West grabbed the remaining broom from the bed of Carter's truck, put two fingers in his mouth and whistled. A black-and-tan dog shot out of the open window of his car. As the dog lolloped up to him, wagging his tail so hard he almost fell over, West looked vaguely embarrassed. "He's a huntaway. Out here that's gotta mean something."

Chapter 12

The phone rang, pulling Dani out of sleep. Blearily, she recognized Becca's voice. There had been another fire, this one at the ostrich facility. John was already there, rounding up ostriches, which had escaped out onto the road and along the beach through cut fences. Becca was on her way with coffee and sandwiches as soon as her mother, who lived on a small cottage on the farm, could come over and mind the children. "Is anyone with you?"

"Like who?" Dani suppressed a yawn, reluctantly alert. With stock on the road it was every landowner's unspoken responsibility to pitch in and help round them up, and in this case some of the stock belonged to her. "Carter?"

"Mm-hmm."

Dani sat bolt upright. "Why?" Although she already knew what Becca was getting at. Jackson's Ridge was a small town and gossip spread like wildfire. Whether she was believed guilty or not, a lot of people had connected her with the crimes.

"If you were sleeping with him that *would* scotch the rumours."

"Well, I'm not." Dani fumbled for the lamp. Golden light flooded the room. "If I ever get the urge again, I'll add that to my list of reasons."

"I know it's none of my business," Becca said bluntly, "but there are plenty of women in Jackson's Ridge who don't need more than one reason, and you used to be one of them."

"Used to." Dani paused in the process of trying to locate her slippers with her toes. Carter and sex—her least favourite subjects. "Hold that thought, it's past tense."

"Maybe. In all the time I've known you—and that's been a few years—he's the only man you've ever slept with."

Dani's stomach sank. "Becca, I've got to go—"

Becca made a strangled sound. "Wait a minute. You were sweet on him *before* he went into the army. You haven't slept with anyone else, have you? Ever. Just Carter."

Dani slid her foot into one slipper, and finally managed to locate the second one. "You make that sound so final."

"I think it might be."

"Well don't spread it around. I'm trying for a little damage control here."

"You mean he doesn't know?"

And she wasn't about to tell him. She couldn't see any reason to hand over that much power to any man, whether she was in love with him or not. "Look, I really have to go."

Suddenly the prospect of chasing down ostriches was a lot more attractive than continuing this particular conversation.

The ostrich farm was a good ten kilometres away by road, but if she used the beach, it was only a twenty-minute ride on horseback. Since she was going to need a horse when she got there, the four-legged method of transport was an easy sell.

Dani changed into riding gear—jeans, short boots and an anorak with reflective stripes. The birds were out on the road, so she needed to be visible. Swiftly, she packed a small knapsack with a flashlight, a bottle of water and a sandwich—in all probability she would be out until dawn.

Minutes later, she'd caught and saddled Elsie, a tall quarter horse bred on the station. She had been Dani's from her birth and was as much a pet as a working horse. Swinging into the saddle, Dani sidled up to the open gate and grabbed the broom she'd propped there. After watching Jim struggle to control the canny, long-necked birds, there was no way she was going near them without an "equalizer."

The moon was out and the ocean was quiet as

Dani let Elsie pick her way down the hill and onto the hard-packed sand above the water line. Even this far away from the fire, the scent of smoke tainted the air. With a gentle squeeze of her knees Dani moved Elsie from a walk to a trot, then let her stretch out into a ground-eating canter. As they neared the end of the long crescent bay, small dark dots appeared on the beach. As Dani got closer, the dots took on shape, half a dozen ostriches moving at a dead run, their white feathers neon-bright in the moonlight.

Dani pulled Elsie in a split second before she jibbed, eyes rolling.

A shudder twitched through Elsie and Dani grinned, holding firm. Cattle from Mars.

Horses didn't like change and ostriches in the moonlight were definitely new.

Dani dropped her voice to a reassuring register. "It's all right girl. They're just skinny cows with long necks. We can take 'em."

If they ran in a herd then they were predictable. With a command, she sent Elsie forward and, brandishing the broom, began working to turn the tiny flock before they split up and scattered past her or moved off the beach and into the manuka scrub. Once they disappeared into the thick low bush they would have a difficult job finding them—let alone getting them out. Wild steers roaming the bush were bad enough—a flock of rogue ostriches didn't bear thinking about.

The birds faltered and slowed to an uneasy halt. Six pairs of glassy eyes stared at her in the moon-

light. Elsie shivered and jibbed again, half rearing.
One of the birds' heads shot up like a periscope. The
ostriches appeared to be equally horrified. A series
of glottal clicks was drowned out by a high-pitched
trill, and with an awkward flurry, the birds turned,
flowing back the way they'd come.

Minutes later, Dani trotted around the curve of
Jackson's Bay onto the stretch of beach that fronted
the ostrich facility. The flashing lights of the fire engine and two police cruisers were visible in the distance, and this close the smell of smoke was acrid.
Ahead, two horsemen—Carter and John McKay—
coalesced out of the darkness, blocking the birds
from running further along the beach and bypassing
the road that led to the facility. The ostriches balked,
then started up the road, wheeling when their path
was blocked by a line of vehicles, and darting
through a gap in the fence where the wire had been
cut and rolled back, making a temporary entrance.

Two men rushed forward and closed the gap.
Dani recognized Pike and Lynch manning the temporary "Taranaki gate," which had been constructed
from wire and battens. Pike fastened the gate and
gestured at Dani's broom. "What's that for? Joust-
ing?"

A voice hollered, "Incoming."

"Necessary equipment." Carter tossed his broom
to Pike.

One of the trucks blocking off the road backed up,
leaving a gap. Seconds later a lone ostrich skittered

through the opening. Lynch scrambled to peel the temporary gate back, Pike lifted the broom and the ostrich's head reared back like a striking snake.

"Put your broom down. It doesn't like it."

The bird's head swivelled in the direction of the disembodied voice. With an angry click it bolted into the paddock.

West materialized out of the gloom. His T-shirt was ripped and a series of red welts was visible on one forearm. Zoom trotted happily at his heels.

West tossed the broom down. "Don't ask." There was always an individual in the pack. It was just his luck he'd been stuck with it.

Half an hour later, the ostriches all tallied and accounted for, Dani tied Elsie up to a fence post well away from the drifting smoke and the flashing lights of the fire engine. John and Carter were in the process of loading the horses into the horse trailer, Becca had opened up the rear of her SUV and was systematically dispensing coffee and sandwiches to the fire crew.

Dani caught the end of a comment about the ostrich farm as she accepted a mug of coffee from Becca. "I didn't know you had an ostrich contract."

Becca shrugged. "It wasn't something John wanted to talk about."

"He's not alone." Pete Barclay loomed out of the darkness, fire helmet in one hand, face smeared with soot.

Dani tensed as Barclay accepted a mug of coffee. The fire that had burned down his barn had been the first in the string of arsons. She'd forgotten he was a volunteer member of the Fire Service.

Barclay glanced at Dani, his expression sour. "A pity you didn't make a better job of it. The shop's gone, but the breeding pens are still intact."

Shock hit Dani like a fist in the chest. Even though she knew she was under suspicion, so far no one, aside from Murdoch, had confronted her openly.

Becca slapped a container of sandwiches down beside Barclay, her jaw set. "There's no need for that. Dani would no more—"

"It's all right, Becca," Dani interjected. Barclay was known for his strongly held opinions and she could understand his anger. In the country there was zero tolerance for anyone who was careless with fire, let alone an arsonist who had lit up in the middle of a drought that carried its own killing power. Generations of work and care—entire livelihoods— could be destroyed within minutes. Barclay hadn't lost everything, but enough to hurt.

Walter Douglas and Pike lined up for coffee and sandwiches, voices roughened by smoke as they thanked Becca and found places to lean or sit. Conversation died a natural death as the men ate and drank, but the silence wasn't companionable. The tension between Barclay and Walter was thick enough to cut, and Dani remembered that Walter's ex-wife was Barclay's sister.

A shrill beeping cut the silence. Walter set down his mug and fished out his pager. He checked the number then stabbed in a short dial on his cell phone as he rose to his feet and disappeared in the direction of the fire truck. Seconds later he walked back into the circle of light. "Dani isn't the arsonist."

Barclay set his mug down, his face grim. "How can you know that?"

A cold voice cut through the conversation. "Logic and plain common sense." Carter loomed out of the darkness. "Dani's a farmer, the same as you, Barclay."

Barclay's face reddened.

Walter looked embarrassed. "Besides that, there's a fire in town. Nola's place—her house this time. Dani couldn't have lit that one unless she has the ability to split herself in two."

Within seconds the fire crew finished loading the hoses and the engine accelerated toward town, leaving the forestry crew to keep a watch on the ostrich facility and dampen down any flare-ups.

Carter's gaze settled on Dani. "Are you all right?"

"Of course she's all right." Becca slapped the lid on the empty sandwich box. "Dani's used to looking after herself—and everyone else. Why would she want a little support just because Barclay thinks she's a hardened criminal?"

Carter handed in his empty mug. "Barclay's an ass. He didn't like losing his barn, and he's got Walter's ex-wife to contend with."

"Tell me about it." Becca screwed the lid onto the coffee pump pot. "Lily decided Walter wasn't good enough for her, and she's been trying to get rid of him ever since. One date with Walter thirty-five years ago and Nola sticks a chastity belt on herself, and all Walter wants is his wife back."

Becca dumped the coffeepot in the picnic hamper wedged into the back of her SUV. Plastic containers of milk and sugar followed. "Some people will do anything for love. Guess that's understandable." Becca turned her sharp gaze on Carter. "Reminds me of another couple I know, not that marriage is involved, although it should have been." The boot came down with a thud.

Carter's head came up with a jerk. Dani's stomach plummeted. Becca's analogy was obscure, but somehow he'd managed to put two and two together.

Face burning, Dani wove through the parked vehicles to where Elsie was tethered. Movement caught her eye, the unnerving sensation of being watched. A shadowy male figure was standing, leaning against a truck.

For a split second the present dissolved and she was thrown back in time to the icy floorboards and bare branches of a South Island winter, the breath locked in her throat and her stomach tight with dread as she watched *him*. She had never found out his name; her mother had always refused to give it to her, saying that giving him even that small dignity made him important, and he wasn't. He was a cowardly worm who should be locked up.

Elsie stamped. Blinking, Dani shook off the eerie moment. With fingers that weren't entirely steady, she unhitched the horse and swung into the saddle, the urgency to be gone increasing with every second.

Carter loomed out of the darkness as Elsie negotiated the ditch and scrambled up onto the road. Dani's jaw set. There was no doubt about it: Carter knew exactly what Becca had been talking about.

He reached for the bridle. "Wait."

Dani kneed Elsie into a trot, eluding his hold. "Later."

When she'd had time to panic, and time to shore up her scattered defences.

As Dani directed Elsie onto the beach she couldn't help reflecting on one salient fact.

Most of the men had stopped to have coffee or a sandwich, with one notable exception. Some time in the last half hour O'Halloran had gone missing.

The beach was quiet, the waves flattened out to a gentle rhythmic wash, the scent of smoke replaced by a cool early-morning tang.

Dani dismounted, prised off her boots, peeled out of her anorak and waded into the water. When she was deep enough, she dove under, letting the salt water wash away the stench of smoke. Refreshed, she waded out, stuffed her boots and anorak in the knapsack and swung back in the saddle. Minutes later, when she reached the home paddock, Elsie nickered, and with a sense of inevitability Dani saw that Carter was waiting.

A shiver coursed down her spine as she dismounted, her shirt clinging to her skin like wet seaweed.

"Why didn't you tell me?"

In a moment of clarity she realised that with Carter she had always been on the defensive; a part of her had been afraid to get that close. He had walked out on her three times, *and she had let him*—his risky career with the SAS an easy out. She had thought he was the one who couldn't commit, but he wasn't alone in that. "I didn't think it would do either of us any good."

His jaw tightened. "I'm not walking away from this."

And, for the first time, she didn't expect him to. Ever since he'd come back she'd been aware that the rules had changed, that what they both wanted had changed.

Always before, she had managed to keep her innermost self apart and intact, but the moment she had realised she was in love with him, that subtle line of defence was gone. She wanted him—the emotion naked and raw. To compound her problem, she hadn't had another relationship with which to compare what she was feeling. Carter was literally her first, last and only.

His expression was grim as he unsaddled Elsie and carried the leathers into the tack room. Dani finished rubbing Elsie down, eased off the halter and watched her amble into her favourite spot in the paddock.

When she turned, Carter was waiting.

Heart pounding, she put her fingers in his. She'd wasted a lot of time and missed a lot of chances through stubbornness and fear; risky or not, she didn't want to miss any more.

Every cell in her body tensed as they walked through the dark, across the paddock that separated the two houses, and into the open doors of his bedroom. Moonlight delineated the bed with its plain, masculine bedspread, the spare lines of dressers, and the faded pattern of an antique rug.

His shirt dropped to the floor. Pale light showed broad shoulders and the sheen of hard muscle and her breath stopped in her throat. Why had she ever thought she could resist him? Instead of kissing her he stepped behind her and began unravelling her hair from its plait. His fingers ran through the thick strands, gradually untangling her hair until it hung in a damp curtain down her back. "*Were* you a virgin the first time we made love?"

"What do you think? There never was anyone else."

His fingers tightened in her hair, pulling her back against his chest and a shaft of heat went through her. She felt his breath on her cheek. "I'm glad Becca said something—now some of it finally makes sense."

Her shirt dropped to the floor. "What do you mean, some of it?"

His arms wound around her waist, pulling her back against him again, the skin-to-skin contact searingly hot after the chill of wet cotton. "The way you are."

His teeth grazed her neck and she bit down on her lip. "I always thought you were the complicated one."

His mouth shifted closer to the lobe of her ear and she tried to concentrate. With a slick move he turned her around in his arms. "There's never been anything complicated about what I want."

The unexpected humour dissolved the constriction in her chest. Letting out a breath, Dani laid her head in the curve between his neck and shoulder, wound her arms around his waist and finally allowed herself to relax. It wasn't as if she didn't know *this*—the closeness and the intimacy that had entwined them for years.

The first kiss was unexpectedly soft, the second even sweeter. Something tickled her forehead. A downy piece of feather drifted onto her nose.

She blew, dislodging it. "Ostriches. Lately, I can't seem to get away from them."

"Forget the ostriches."

Carter walked her across the room. The back of her knees hit the bed. She sat down, pulling Carter with her.

"Wait."

His expression was rueful as he straightened. A drawer slid open. Dani glanced at the bedside table. Beside the box of condoms was a handgun.

She stared at the sleek, metallic shape. Despite being around guns most of her life, the reality was shocking. The weapons she was used to seeing were the ones farmers used for pest control—usually a twenty-two rifle of some description kept locked in a cabinet—not stashed beside the bed. The weapon was an abrupt reminder of what Carter did for a living.

She caught the gleam of his smile. "Sorry. Habit."

She noticed there was another piece of equipment beyond the gun, but she couldn't quite make out what that was.

He slipped off his jeans and for the first time she saw the mass of scar tissue on his thigh. If she needed a reminder that she had come close to losing him permanently, that was it.

"Come here."

Anticipation shivered through her as he unhooked her bra and peeled off her damp jeans. Fully dressed, Carter was impressive—naked he was enough to stop any red-blooded woman's heart.

His mouth came down on hers and the night began to dissolve. He was being careful, treating her as if she was made of porcelain, but she didn't want his restraint. Winding her arms around his neck, Dani lifted up on her toes and kissed him back, arching into him. He felt hot and male against her and vitally alive. She had almost lost him, but he was here—now—and, for the moment at least, he was hers.

The moon had set and the sky was lightening in the east as Dani finally drifted into sleep. Carter's arm came around her in a familiar gesture, tucking her in against him. Sleepily, she adjusted her position until she was comfortable.

They had fallen asleep that way countless times, but in the sleepy aftermath of making love it reminded her of the first time they had ever shared a bed. For Dani the experience had been utterly new, the relief of being held almost unbearable after the grief of losing both Susan and Robert.

After months of absence, Carter had been there when she'd needed him most, taking over the farm and shielding her from the curiosity that had surrounded the double tragedy. He'd helped her through the ordeal of the inquest and the legal tangle of the will. The fact that he'd also provided a shoulder to cry on had broken through her barriers; after years of carefully avoiding intimacy her guard had been down.

Both eyes popped open. In a moment of clarity, she recognized what she'd always refused to see.

Six years ago, Carter had stepped in when she was grieving and at her most vulnerable. After years of successfully avoiding intimacy she'd fallen into his arms like a ripe plum.

Several weeks later, he had had to go back to barracks and the imbalance in the relationship had been established.

Despite the absences and three breakups, she hadn't dated anyone but Carter since they had first started going out together. Men had looked, but none of them had ever asked her out. She'd noticed the restraint, but it hadn't bothered her because she simply hadn't wanted anyone else. She was now certain that Carter had made sure any male within a radius of fifty miles knew she belonged to him, and the campaign wasn't confined to men. The entire township of Jackson's Ridge already behaved as if she and Carter were married.

The extent of Carter's control sent a shiver down her spine. She had thought he had changed since he'd come back, and she'd attributed the changes to the ordeal he'd gone through in Indonesia, but she had been wrong. The ruthless streak was an intrinsic part of Carter; he had been like that all along.

* * *

The room was washed with sunlight when the phone rang. Carter picked up, the conversation brief and monosyllabic.

"Murdoch." He put the phone down, leaned over and kissed her on the mouth. "I promised to meet him."

Dani's drowsiness evaporated as Carter walked into the bathroom. The drumming of the shower cut out further conversation. When Carter walked out, already half-dressed and looking for a fresh shirt she sat bolt upright, the sheet wrapped around her breasts. "What does he want?"

"To talk about the arsonist."

"Then I should be there."

Carter shrugged into a shirt. "He just wants to go through some profiling information."

"Then he must have a suspect."

He paused in the act of fastening his shirt. "He's keeping an eye on someone, but all he has is speculation—nothing solid."

She lifted an eyebrow. "You mean he's trying to keep me out of it."

He bent and kissed her on the mouth. "The hell with Murdoch. *I* want to keep you out of it. Besides, John mentioned last night that you've got a brunch date."

Dani blinked, feeling abruptly disoriented. It was Sunday. With everything that had happened—disaster piling on top of disaster—it felt like a month had passed since she had promised to go to Becca's brunch, not just a few days.

Chapter 13

Murdoch poured fresh coffee into his mug, sat down at his desk, booted up his computer and eased into the one day the police station should have been closed. He had been in Jackson's Ridge for going on twenty years. When he'd started out in enforcement, he'd been a city cop. Moving to the country had been like a breath of fresh air. He'd married one of the local girls, had kids, and gradually fitted into the community. When he retired he planned to stay here. But as much as he loved Jackson's Ridge, he hated it when the small-town thing went a little crazy on him.

Hardened criminals and stupid kids he could understand, their motivations were straightforward, but investigating ordinary citizens—people he knew and saw most days—made his stomach queasy. It was like ripping the lid off a trash can. In the light of day, nothing looked good.

The sound of the front door creaking jerked Murdoch's head up. Coldly, he eyed the two men who strolled into the field room. Carter he'd expected, but not Marc O'Halloran. "What are you two doing here?"

O'Halloran's gaze was openly curious as he looked around the tiny police station. "I've got withdrawal. Just wanted to breathe in the scent of crimes being solved."

Murdoch didn't fight to keep the sour expression off his face. "I've done some checking. Your psychological profile isn't the best." He clicked on his screen saver. "Way I heard it, you might be a cop, but in the last case you worked your methods bordered on the criminal."

O'Halloran studied an open file on Murdoch's desk. "I prefer the word unconventional."

Murdoch closed the file. "Either way, you're not sticking your nose into this investigation. According to Auckland Central, you're on leave until you get some perspective back."

O'Halloran hooked up a chair and sat down. "Thing is, I can help you."

He leaned forward and pointed at a map of Jackson's Bay Murdoch had spread out on one end of his desk. "Lately I've noticed traffic along the beach road, always at night, and with no lights. I've had a look around, and no one's fishing or swimming. The vehicle gets parked—" he indicated a position on the map "—there."

Carter's gaze narrowed. O'Halloran had just pinpointed the location he had found and relayed to Murdoch. "It's a four-wheel drive. There's a track leading up the hill to Dani's place."

O'Halloran sat back. "Have you gotten a visual?"

Carter propped himself on the corner of the desk and set a small gear bag he was carrying on the floor. "Not yet."

The front of Murdoch's chair hit the floor with a snap. "Wait just one minute. If I let you in on this, you follow orders, and Ray Cornell—or anyone else at Auckland Central—doesn't hear a whisper."

O'Halloran showed the first trace of animation. "As far as I'm concerned I didn't come in here today."

"Good." Murdoch shoved a calendar across the desk. "There is a pattern to it. And somehow Dani is connected to almost every crime. The first fire was Barclay's, and that was a couple of weeks back. Pete's wife, Sybil, had a physiotherapy appointment with Dani."

"Maybe that fire isn't part of the pattern."

"The same accelerant was used. The likelihood that we're dealing with different offenders is remote."

"So what do we have, aside from Dani Marlow and the accelerant, that's solid?"

Murdoch's expression turned grim. "Since last night's fire, a long list of suspects—all of them with ostrich contracts—and the fact that Walter Douglas got to the Barclay fire early. According to one of the volunteers, he was warming up the engine when he got the call."

"And this." Carter opened up the bag and pulled out a plastic bag containing a canister. "I've been checking for theft, but instead I found an empty tin of accelerant in Dani's barn this morning. It wasn't there yesterday."

Murdoch's jaw tightened. "Which means it was placed there last night, *after* the ostrich facility went up. I'll have to get it to Mason. It'll take a day, but I'm willing to bet that if this is a set-up, we won't find any prints."

An hour later, with a plan in place, O'Halloran rose to his feet. He paused at the door to reception and eyed Carter. "Heard you worked with Cornell on a couple of cases, but I didn't expect to see you doing police work in Jackson's Ridge. But then, correct me if I'm wrong, you two are related, right?"

Murdoch muttered something dire beneath his breath as O'Halloran walked out, whistling.

When O'Halloran was gone Carter pulled up a chair and sat beside Murdoch. "Don't worry about the nepotism thing, he'll never use it."

The computer screen glowed bright blue as Murdoch clicked on the mouse. "You were right, Susan Marlow has a file, but not the usual kind."

Seconds later the file flashed up on the computer. Carter leaned over his shoulder and stared at the screen. The first complaint was dated twenty-four years ago, the last just two years later. "That's three complaints she logged in three different towns. Two breaking and entering, the last one detailing a serious assault."

"All three complaints withdrawn, no conviction obtained, and after that…nothing."

Murdoch tried another check, then another, but after the date of the final complaint nothing further had been lodged.

Carter studied the name of the offender supplied in the first two complaints, Jordan Carlisle. The third, more serious complaint was listed as an unknown offender and it had been lodged by a neighbour, not Susan Marlow. "Any idea who this guy is?"

Murdoch frowned he did a search on Carlisle, but drew a blank. "A dead end. Figures. The computer files only go back so many years. If I want the file, I'll have to request it."

"Do it."

Murdoch folded his arms across his chest. "I don't need you to tell me what to do. I'm not in one of your death squads."

Carter reached for patience. "The SAS doesn't run death squads—that was in the Second World War."

Murdoch gave him a hard-assed look. "Really?"

Carter clamped down on his temper. "Are you getting the file?"

Murdoch tapped out an e-mail and pressed the send button. "What do you think?"

Carter headed for the door. "You don't want to know."

He knew the approximate date when Dani and her mother had turned up in Jackson's Ridge, but that left a four-year gap since the date of the last complaint. Four years in which they had disappeared off the scope.

The facts weren't conclusive; just because Susan Marlow had never lodged another complaint that didn't mean they were on the run, but for Carter a final, vital piece of the puzzle had just dropped into place. He had worked undercover operations for years, he knew how to disappear, and he was certain that was what Susan and Dani had done. He knew from what his mother had let drop that Susan Marlow had been hiding from something. When Susan and Dani had first arrived in Jackson's Ridge their possessions had amounted to little more than a couple of suitcases and a car, and for the first few months Susan had refused to use charge accounts, insisting on paying for everything in cash. If his calculations were correct they had spent at least four years on the run, and more probably six.

He was finally beginning to understand why Dani was so hard to reach. If the man who was stalking them was who he thought it was, it was no wonder she had a fundamental distrust of relationships and men.

Dani heard the truck before it pulled up out in front of the house. Albert Docherty, the owner of an antiques shop in Mason, jumped out of the passenger seat and jerked his head at the two men with him. Dani took him through the house, pointing out the furniture that was to go while the driver of the truck reversed and backed as close to the front steps as he could get.

Docherty eyed the furniture in the master bedroom with a pleased look. After a brief inspection, he handed a cheque to Dani. "This stuff doesn't come on the market very often. Shouldn't have any problem selling it."

With a curt nod, he motioned his men to start packing the pieces. The process took time, as every drawer and mirror had to be removed and wrapped, and the bed was ornate enough to be a difficult proposition to dismantle, let alone lift.

Dani watched as the rooms emptied out. The men were pleasant and professional, but it didn't change the fact that she was losing something precious. When the last piece was gone, the house felt bare and hollow. She'd kept the furniture in her room and David's, one couch in the lounge and the kitchen table and chairs. The family portraits and paintings still hung on the walls. David had wanted to sell them, but there was no market for portraits, just the frames. For the tiny sum they'd realize selling the frames, Dani had decided David could afford to keep that link to the past.

The man lifted binoculars to his eyes and watched the final piece of furniture being loaded. A pity it all didn't stay in the house, but that didn't matter. Satisfaction curled in the pit of his stomach. The plan was proceeding. He wanted to see Dani lose the way he had lost. Slowly, bit-by-bit, piece-by-piece, her life ground away until she had nothing.

Dani studied her bank statement in the glow of light from her desk lamp, reached for the calculator and ran some figures. When she was finished, she sat back in her chair and ran shaky fingers through her hair. Once she banked the cheque for the furniture and for David's car the account would fatten up, but not enough. She would have to find something else to sell. On Galbraith the only thing of value left was the breeding herd.

Pushing back her chair she rose to her feet and walked down the hall, leaving the house by the nearer exit of the back porch instead of her usual route through the kitchen. Grimly, she drank in the balmy air and stared at the spectacle of diamond-bright stars and a night sky so clear it looked like black glass. The clarity meant there was little moisture in the air, and no likelihood of any soon. The endless hot days and nights were sucking the station dry. Today the number-two well had dried up, which meant she'd had to move the cattle from the back block of the station in closer to the house. The move meant more pressure on the grass, and more feeding out of precious winter food.

When David saw the state of the paddocks he was going to throw a fit. Some were little more than dust, and would have to be resown. The paddocks that had fared better had only done so because they were infested with weeds and overrun with the native kikuyu grass that had the advantage of being hardy but was low on nutritional values. Those paddocks, too, would have to be resown.

The Galbraith bad-luck streak was in full flight, and it didn't look like giving up any time soon.

Dani stared through the trees toward Carter's house. It was in darkness, which meant that wherever he'd gone, he still hadn't come back.

Taking a deep breath, Dani turned to walk back into the house when something shimmered at the edge of her vision.

Adrenaline pumped. A hoot, just metres from where she was standing, resonated through the night. Something floated, eerie and silent overhead. Letting out a breath, Dani forced herself to relax. A morepork.

Shaking her head, she skimmed the expanse of lawn and the dark shrubs that edged it. She frowned. Something had moved—a rearrangement of the shadows that couldn't be explained by a nonexistent breeze or the soundless flight of a morepork.

Seconds ticked by as she waited and watched. A chilled certainty gripped the back of her neck. Someone or something was out there.

Stepping inside, she grabbed a flashlight then, with a soft tread, she threaded her way through the trees until she reached Carter's house.

She knocked on the door, but she was already certain he wasn't home—his truck wasn't parked in the garage—then stepped inside.

Feeling like a thief, she walked through to his bedroom, flicked on the flashlight and slid the drawer of his bedside table open. The handgun was missing, but it was the other item she was interested in.

She stared at the contraption. Now that she could see it fully, it was easily identifiable. She'd read enough about Special Forces to understand the kind of work they did and some of the equipment they used. These were night-vision goggles.

Slipping the goggles from the drawer, she slid it closed, flicked off the flashlight and slipped outside.

She examined the night-vision gear. There was no manual, but how difficult could it be? Flipping the power button, she slipped them over her head. Instantly, Carter's front yard sprang to life in shades of a ghostly, luminous green.

Satisfaction took the edge off her tension. She wasn't hunting a prowler who could possibly be the arsonist terrorising Jackson's Ridge, she was just checking out her place. Something was lurking around. It was most likely a stray cat or dog, in which case she was more likely to see it at night. If it was a person...

Her stomach tightened at the possibility. If there *was* a prowler, at least then she would know and she could do something about it.

Adjusting the fit, she stepped off the veranda and merged with the shrubs at the edge of the lawn. It took a few moments to get used to the feel of the goggles and the surreal cast they gave to the landscape.

She could see perfectly as long as she was looking directly ahead, the problem was with her peripheral vision. In order to widen her field of vision, she needed to constantly move her head from side to side.

Keeping to the edge of the lawn, she began walking, first of all reconnoitring around her house and the barn, then widening the circle to include the groves of trees and the paddocks immediately surrounding the house.

The crunch of a snapped twig jerked her head around. Something moved, dissolving into the bush line. A branch quivered, as if it had been pushed aside and had just flicked back into place and the marrow in her spine froze. Whatever had passed through the trees was too large to be either a cat or dog.

For long minutes she stayed still and silent, straining to listen, but with the faint breeze that had begun sifting through the treetops it was difficult to pick up the subtler sounds.

A rustling in the shrubs behind made her freeze. He must have doubled around.

Adrenaline pumping, she didn't question her automatic assertion that whoever had made the noise was human and male as she spun—and stumbled into the hard wall of a chest. A hand closed over her mouth, muffling the small sound that erupted.

"If you press that button, it goes to thermal."

The image changed. Carter's outline took on a yellowish glow.

Slowly, he released her. "Depending on the ambient light, sometimes it's better to switch to thermal, but in your case..." He removed the goggles from her head. "The less you know the better. The idea that you're out here in the dark stalking a prowler makes me crazy."

"I wasn't stalking anything. I was just...looking."

"Next time you have the urge to 'look,' make it go away. When did you get the goggles?"

"A few minutes ago."

"Sneaky. I never even checked on them until tonight."

Beneath the surge of embarrassment at being caught out, her interest sharpened. If he wanted the goggles tonight, that meant he was up to something. "I didn't think you were home. I didn't hear your truck."

"That's because it's parked down the road."

"Something *is* going on."

His hand closed over hers. "That's why you have to come with me now."

Chapter 14

The sound of a vehicle was audible above the steady roar of the surf. Despite the fact that the lights were off, the truck was clearly visible as it turned left, away from the beach and went off road. Seconds later the engine sound died.

Dani stayed crouched on the side of the hill, watching as dark figures converged on the lone man exiting the truck. A spotlight flicked on, flooding the area with light.

Murdoch's voice was incredulous. "Walter?"

Walter Douglas straightened, shaking off Carter's hand. "What is all this? I was just down for a little fishing—"

"I suppose that's why you concealed your truck in that patch of scrub back there."

"I'd be a fool to leave it out in the open. Someone might steal my tires."

Murdoch looked around. "Who, Walter? You're on private land and Jackson's Ridge isn't exactly a hotbed of crime. Until lately, that is."

"I don't believe in taking chances."

Murdoch let out a breath. "Okay, let's go and look at your truck, and while you're at it, you can show me your fishing rod, and explain why exactly you're going fishing when the tide's out. If there's anything bigger than a sprat out there I'll shoot myself."

Walter turned on his heel. "I've got a fishing rod."

"I'll just bet you do."

Dani stared at Walter's retreating back and the four officers flanking him. She felt charged for action and oddly deflated. She couldn't believe the fire chief was the culprit, but that had definitely been Walter.

A few minutes later, Carter and Murdoch approached the small hide where Dani had been told to wait. Murdoch was apologetic. "I've taken Walter into custody. He had a jar of fire-lighting gel in his truck. There's no way that can be explained away on night-fishing. He says he doesn't know how the gel came to be in his fishing tackle…" He shook his head. "He won't admit it, but it's him all right. I talked to his ex-wife this afternoon and she's confirmed that she saw Walter prowling around the Barclay place several days before the first fire. The fact that he's out here below your house explains a lot. According to Lily, Robert Galbraith was instrumental in persuading Walter to buy shares in the ostrich facility." Murdoch shrugged. "He denies wanting revenge, and the motivation is a little murky, but it's adding up."

Tail lights winked as the cruisers disappeared into the night. Walter's truck was left where it was parked, a length of crime tape surrounding it fluttering in the breeze.

Carter unhooked one of the ropes from around the trunk of a tree. He slung the coil over one shoulder. "Looks like that's it. Let's go home."

O'Halloran slipped the folded net they hadn't had to use into a long, black gear bag. "Seemed too easy."

Gabriel West, who had travelled down from Auckland to help with the bust, zipped the bag closed and hefted it. "That's because it was. I felt sorry for him."

O'Halloran hefted the second coil of rope. "No weapon. And he had a limp."

Absently Dani listened to the banter that flowed between Carter and West. More of the same only in different locations: Afghanistan, Iraq, Papua New Guinea—anywhere and everywhere there'd been some kind of conflict. The camaraderie that flowed between them was as relaxed and intimate as if they were members of the same family. She'd read the Mars and Venus stuff. Men and women were different, but she wasn't just dealing with the male/female thing here—these guys lived in another universe completely.

Carter's hand landed in the small of her back. Automatically, she began to move forward, matching his stride. Dark shadows flowed on either side of her. As they walked she couldn't help but notice the absence of noise beneath the muted sound of the waves. Even though there was no need they all still stepped carefully, as if the habit was ingrained and, despite the fact that climbing the steep slope was heavy going, there was no evidence of exertion; every one of them was fit. A faint chill—an aftermath of the tension that had gripped her while she'd lain, concealed in the scrub—gripped her spine. She felt as though she was walking up the hill with a pack of wolves.

A man dressed in dark clothing lay flattened against the gnarled branch of an ancient pohutukawa tree as he followed the progress of the small group. When they disappeared from sight, he waited for a few minutes, listening to the waves and letting the night sounds sink in until he was sure he was alone.

Quietly, he inched along the limb, climbed down the squat, twisted trunk and, with a soft tread, retreated into the hills.

The *Jackson's Ridge Chronicle* was out. Walter had been charged, referred for a psychiatric evaluation and released on bail pending a court hearing.

Flynn was relieved. The mid-week edition had achieved its highest-ever recorded circulation—carrying the paper out of the red for the first time in months. The residents of Jackson's Ridge were happy. Murdoch wasn't.

He dropped a copy of the *Chronicle* on Carter's desk. "Walter's only admitted to one of the fires, the Barclay's barn. Unfortunately, that's the only one we can tie him to."

Carter studied the story. Like Murdoch, he hadn't been comfortable with Walter's arrest. Walter just didn't have the personality aberrations of a serial arsonist. "Which means there's a copycat. Has Walter got any idea who the other arsonist is?"

Murdoch picked up his coffee, stared at the dregs and set it back down. "That's where it gets a little complicated. Walter was supposedly meeting the real arsonist on the beach. He claims it's the first time he's been there for anything but fishing for months. He said he received a typewritten note and that the real arsonist must have planted the gel in with his fishing gear. If he's telling the truth then *he's* been set up."

"Don't tell me. He doesn't have the note."

"He burnt it." Murdoch shrugged. "Walter's scared. Whoever the second arsonist is, he threatened to burn down Walter's house and business if he didn't show. If Walter loses the butcher shop, his income's gone."

"Is that an issue when he's going to do time?"

"The Barclays don't want to press charges. Walter's been a part of their family for thirty-five years, so that's understandable. And Lily's blaming herself for the fire. Apparently, until she walked out on Walter, he didn't have a clue that she wasn't happy." Murdoch shrugged. "Providing we don't turn up anything else it looks like all Walter will face is a hefty bill for damages and the emergency call-outs."

The flash of sunlight on rich auburn hair caught Carter's eye, then the graceful swing of Dani's long-legged gait as she strolled in the direction of Nola's café. There was only one woman in Jackson's Ridge who looked like that—or anywhere, for that matter. Dani was distinctive. Like Susan Marlow, wherever she went she would always attract attention. "What about Carlisle?"

That name again. Aside from the fact that Jordan Carlisle was a wealthy stockbroker with heavy-duty connections in the business world, he was also Dani's father.

Murdoch unearthed a file and dropped it in front of Carter. "It came in by courier this morning. Interesting reading."

Interesting was an understatement. Jordan Rayburn Carlisle, eldest son of the wealthy and influential Carlisle family, had started out in life with a silver spoon in his mouth. A brilliant student, he had achieved a law degree with honours and had been poised to progress into a partnership in the family law firm. Instead, he had ended up in prison, disbarred and banned from taking any part in the family business—doing time for grievous bodily harm and the attempted murder of his unborn child, Danielle Margaret Marlow.

Carter's jaw tightened as he skimmed the details. Carlisle had dated Susan Marlow, a legal secretary with his firm, gotten her pregnant then demanded she have an abortion. When Susan had refused, he had hit her in the abdomen in a deliberate attempt to make the foetus abort. Susan's landlord had heard the ruckus and intervened, and had sustained a broken jaw and a hairline fracture to the skull for his trouble. The police had picked Carlisle up and he'd been remanded on bail, Susan had ended up in hospital and almost lost the baby. The intimidation had continued, but she had stuck to her guns and indicted him. Carlisle had gone down for eight years, six of which he had served.

The file finished there, but Carter could fill in the blanks for himself. When Carlisle had gotten out of jail, his career and position in the family firm gone, he had gone after Susan and Dani. He had stalked them, driving them from town to town, until, in desperation, and in fear of their lives, Susan had stopped reporting the harassment and had simply concentrated on disappearing. When Susan had decided to stay in Jackson's Ridge she had taken a huge risk. With the resources available to Jordan Carlisle she'd had to know it was only a matter of time before he found them.

Carter's gaze was cold. "Where is he?"

Murdoch steepled his fingers. "He's disappeared. Hasn't been seen at his inner-city apartment for weeks."

But there were no prizes for guessing where Carlisle was. The only thing Carter couldn't figure out was how he'd managed to stay hidden. In a small place like Jackson's Ridge, the second a stranger drove into town, it was news.

Dani walked into Nola's café. Becca was waiting, a copy of the *Jackson's Ridge Chronicle* spread out on the table.

Nola, busy cleaning off a nearby table, paused to set a menu in front of her. "Hear Carter's back to barracks tomorrow."

Dani pulled out a chair and sat down. "He's got his final medical."

"Expect they'll be shipping him back out to Indonesia. There's been a lot of trouble there."

Dani kept her expression noncommittal as she ordered coffee. "Your guess is as good as mine."

But all the same, the knowledge that he was leaving Jackson's Ridge at all was an old trigger and hard to shake. They were sleeping together—the intimacy she'd worked so hard at avoiding had caught her off guard and tipped her life upside down—but in every other respect nothing about their relationship had changed.

Becca frowned at Nola's retreating back. "Don't listen. She's still upset that you could have even thought about turning Carter down."

"It's okay." And surprisingly enough, despite Nola's occasional sharpness, it was. Dani was aware there was no malice in the exchange, just the worn-in familiarity of years. Nola had known Carter since he was a baby. She'd seen him grow up, she'd known his parents and his grandparents, and still kept in touch with Carter's mother. They weren't related by blood, but to Nola, Carter was family.

Becca folded the paper and put it to one side. "Has Carter proposed?"

For the barest moment Dani's heart stopped in her chest. She hadn't known until that moment how much she wanted not just a proposal, but the whole deal—marriage, babies and family. The hunger had sneaked up on her, a silent ambush that had swept the ground from beneath her feet. "Not lately."

"He won't walk out on you again." Becca's expression was fierce.

"No," Dani agreed, "he won't." She stared at the menu. Now that she was head over heels in love with him, her tolerance level had shrunk to zero. If he left again, that would be it; she couldn't afford to have him in her life in any capacity. Staying away wouldn't be just a simple case of protection, it would be a requirement for survival.

Becca lifted her brows, openly fishing for some kind of admission. *"And?"*

"And nothing." Dani waited until Nola had set their coffee down on the table and left. "You know me."

"Uh-huh. The last thing you committed to was taking over where Robert Galbraith left off. Ever since then you've been on hold. When are you going to let go of that place? David's got to be, what? Seventeen?"

"Eighteen." Dani sipped her coffee and set the cup back on its saucer. "I'll let go when the cattle are sold and the mortgage is paid."

And not a second before. Quite apart from the fact that she loved her brother, she owed it to David—and to Susan and Robert—to hang on.

"I just hope Carter stays around that long."

"What makes you think he's even coming back after he's pronounced fit?"

"Call it women's intuition." Becca shook her head. "You know, sometimes I could shake you. You're one of the smartest women I know, but you can't see what's going on right under your nose."

A flicker of movement drew Dani's attention. On the other side of the trellis that enclosed the outdoor seating area she could see Nola talking to a man. A split second later Nola lifted up on tiptoe and kissed him on the mouth.

Dani looked away, faintly embarrassed that she'd witnessed the scene. "Tell me that wasn't Walter."

Becca picked up her coffee. "It's Walter. Nola rang John up last night to tell him the news. They're dating."

"Since when?"

"Since the fire at her house." Becca shrugged. "Nola won't admit to anything, but rumour is that she lit the fire solely to get his attention—which she did."

As Dani lifted her cup to her mouth and sipped, Carter's truck slotted into a parking space outside the café.

Becca watched his progress as he locked the truck and stepped up on the curb. "Speak of the devil…."

Dani tensed. There was no doubt that Carter looked good. Female heads automatically turned when he walked by. Her spine stiffened as a familiar voice called out. She spotted Mia sitting at a shady table with Roger Wells. The last she'd heard, Mia was just passing through—on her way to pick apples in Nelson. Either she'd never made it out of town or she was back for another visit.

Carter lifted a hand, but didn't change direction and Dani breathed a sigh of relief. She'd never thought of herself as a jealous woman—another of the changes she was slowly adjusting to.

Nola appeared as he took the seat next to Dani. Within seconds a glass of ice water was deposited in front of him.

Absently, Dani listened to the way he answered Nola's queries. Not for the first time she noticed there was nothing flirtatious or over-friendly about Carter's manner or his replies, he was decidedly low-key. Despite that reticence, the female sex gravitated to him—whether they were eight or eighty. The machismo aside, they simply liked him.

Nola tucked her tray under one arm. "When are you leaving?"

Carter's gaze caught hers. "Tomorrow night."

Dani kept her expression blank. A few minutes later, Carter helped her into the truck. She felt edgy and aware and fragile, and more inclined to argue than make nice conversation. "Where are we going?"

"Home."

The word carried more poignancy than usual. *One more day*. She couldn't help it; she had a sense of foreboding.

Chapter 15

Dani rose in the pre-dawn darkness. Rex, David's gelding, nickered and trotted along behind her as she caught Elsie. A cool breeze blew in off the ocean as she led the mare out of the paddock, bringing with it the smell of salt and ozone and blowing away the last dregs of sleep. Suppressing a shiver, she rubbed the old mare's nose as she slipped off the halter, slotted the bridle over her head and fitted the bit in her mouth. "Last time girl, then you can retire."

They both could. After this she would be packing her bags. When David came back, she intended either to move her practice into Jackson's Ridge, or make a fresh start in Mason. For most of her life her home had been at Galbraith, but now that time was over. Whether she succeeded or failed to meet the mortgage, it was past time to strike out on her own. The challenge both invigorated and scared her, but the reasoning was sound.

Becca had been right: it was time to let go. She was thirty years old, and for the past six years she had been running on guilt. Once David moved back to Galbraith it wouldn't take long for him to settle into a relationship and start a family and when that happened, Dani intended to be long gone. There was no way she was going to play gooseberry in her brother's marriage.

Minutes later Dani cinched the saddle tight, swung up and squeezed her calves against Elsie's flanks, although she hardly needed to urge the old mare on. Elsie was a stock horse born and bred, she might be close on sixteen, but she loved to work. Her ears pricked as she started forward at a brisk amble, automatically heading through the gate.

Dani checked the luminous dial of her watch. The truck was due at ten, which gave her five hours to get the cattle into the stockyards. Most of the herd was already in close, it wouldn't take much to move them, but Murphy's Law held for farming just like it did for everything else. There was always a difficult one in the bunch. In this case she could guarantee it was going to be Buster. Buster had been a headstrong calf and a difficult yearling. Neutering hadn't seemed to make much difference; he still thought he was in charge.

As Elsie ambled on, the echo of hooves became more distinct, then separated into two sets of hoof-

beats. A sense of inevitability gripped her as a rider
materialised out of the mist. It was Carter up on
Rex. He must have caught and saddled him just minutes after she'd ridden out.

An ache started in her chest as he came abreast.
"I thought you were leaving today."

"I changed the appointment."

By lunchtime the cattle, including the breeding
herd, were mustered into the stockyards, ready to be
trucked to the sale. Two hours later, dust hung in the
air as the last truck pulled away, leaving the pens,
and the farm, empty.

Emotion gripped Dani as the roar of the last truck
receded to be replaced by silence. She had the stron-
gest sensation that the pulse that was Galbraith had
just stopped. She had been prepared to feel empty,
but she hadn't expected to feel grief. Over the years
the high, windy plateau and coastal strip had made
a place for itself in her heart. It was home.

As they rode back to the house a curious calmness settled on her. She would still have to wait on
the sale prices to see if there was enough to meet the
balloon payment. Win or lose, she had done her best.
If that wasn't good enough, she couldn't change it
now.

The night was hot and close, most of the stars
blanked out by cloud, as a vehicle idled along the
dusty farm roads that crisscrossed the Rawlings
property and provided access to the long peninsula

that curved out into the sea and formed the northern-most point of Jackson's Bay. The road angled in close to the beach before downgrading to little more than a goat track, but Carlisle wasn't interested in reaching the peninsula.

Bringing the truck to a halt in the lee of a small dune, he slipped a knapsack on his back and struck out across country toward the Rawlings place, keeping to the cover of scrubby manuka, stunted by salt and bent and twisted toward land by perpetual sea winds. Satisfied that he had taken every precaution to elude Marc O'Halloran, who had almost caught him on a couple of occasions, he paused in the deep shadow of a lone pohutukawa, allowing himself several minutes to adjust to the night sounds. When he was satisfied he was alone, he threaded his way up the slope, keeping his steps slow and deliberate.

A half moon emerged from behind a sullen bank of cloud and the bulk of the Rawlings homestead sprang into prominence. Keeping clear of the house, he skirted the shadows, waiting patiently for the cloud to blank out the moon. Rawlings was gone for the night, but that didn't mean he would take unnec-essary risks.

A heavy patch of cloud slid across the moon. Sat-isfied that he was close to invisible, he drifted be-tween the outbuildings, comfortable with the night.

Dani climbed the shell path that led from the beach to her house. Carter had left shortly after the muster, but even though she knew he was only gone for one night, the fact that he was back in barracks didn't make her happy.

Moonlight slanted over Carter's house as she stepped up onto the lawn. She studied the luminous dial of her wristwatch. It was just after eleven. She'd walked for an hour, trying to wear herself out in the hope that she'd simply fall asleep, but the remedy hadn't worked, she didn't feel even remotely tired. After months of being alone, it had only taken days to get used to being one half of a couple again. She *missed* Carter.

Corrosive anger ate at Carlisle as he watched Dani stroll beneath the trees, feet and legs bare, long hair trailing down her back, as if she'd just enjoyed a leisurely stroll along the beach. In the fitful light her resemblance to Susan was uncanny.

Hunkering down in the deep well of shadow cast by an old oak, he set himself to wait, letting the rhythmic sound of the surf on the beach below soothe away the eruption of temper. A few minutes later her bedroom light went out. He gave it ten more minutes then he rose to his feet and strolled along the edge of the lawn toward the house.

Fifteen minutes later he crawled beneath the house and extracted dry strips of kindling, newspaper, a lighter, and a container of fire gel from his knapsack. Petrol or white spirits were more volatile, and normally he got a kick out of the explosion, but in this case he needed to keep the noise level down. The surf provided a level of background noise that would hide the initial sound of the flames, but not for long, and the last thing he wanted to do was alert Dani.

He watched as the flames consumed the kindling then fed the fire with larger wood he'd found on the woodpile. A burst of blue-white flame spat a glowing ember out of the centre of the fire into a drift of dried leaves. Instantly flames shimmered to life.

Grabbing his knapsack, he retreated from the small blaze and coldly assessed the weather conditions. The usual sea breeze had dropped, leaving the night disappointingly still. The lack of wind and the boxed-in position he'd built the fire in—set where the house bellied low to the ground—would slow the fire but, all the same, once it took hold it would be spectacular.

Picking up his knapsack, and checking the ground in case he'd left anything behind that could incriminate him, he backed into the shadows. This fire was an exception to the rule.

This one he wanted to watch.

Carter strolled through his darkened house, waiting for Murdoch to call. He had ostensibly left town this afternoon, calling in at the supermarket on his way to make sure the message that he'd gone back to barracks was clear. If Carlisle was going to show his hand, it would be tonight.

He hadn't told Dani. As certain as Carter was that Carlisle was the arsonist, so far all he and Murdoch had was supposition. They didn't have one evidential link that connected Carlisle to the Jackson's Ridge arsons. He'd tossed up and decided that with five police officers and himself surveilling the property, Dani didn't need to know that it was possible the man who had stalked her and Susan when she was a child was back in Jackson's Ridge until *after* they'd apprehended him.

The phone rang. Murdoch and Lowell were on stand-by down on the beach road, the two Mason cops were watching Dani's driveway, O'Halloran was watching the beach.

Dani kicked the cotton sheet, her only covering, aside. The polished wooden boards were cool on her feet as she padded across the room to switch the ceiling fan on. Normally, she would simply push her French doors open and let the night air circulate through the house, but Carter had insisted that while he was away, she secure the house. Every window was latched, every door locked, and had been ever since she'd left the house earlier on in the evening. Consequently, the old homestead with its tin roof and lack of ventilating windows was as hot and airless as an oven.

The steady hum as the blades stirred the air provided more comfort than relief; it didn't cool the air so much as move it around.

Sliding back into bed, Dani punched the pillow into shape and made herself comfortable. She needed to sleep, but it was hard to relax when the relationship she needed was slipping through her fingers—for the fourth time.

When Carter had left for barracks she'd recognized the remote quality in his gaze: she'd seen the look often enough.

Her head lifted off the pillow. For long seconds she listened, but the hum of the fan drowned out everything but the distant cry of a pukeko—one of the swamp birds that inhabited the marsh down on the river flat. Punching the pillow again, she forced herself to relax.

It must be her imagination, but it seemed to be getting hotter.

Carter's phone rang again. O'Halloran had spotted a vehicle concealed at the far end of the beach. At first he hadn't been overly alarmed, because the truck was parked some distance away, at the opposite end of the beach, on the track that led out to the peninsula. Locals who were serious about fishing and owned four-wheel-drive vehicles used the track on occasion. And this particular vehicle was familiar; it belonged to a neighbour.

Carter tensed, all of his instincts on alert. The Galbraith roads were being watched; not his. The omission had been a calculated risk. Murdoch only had so much manpower, and they were already stretched thin covering the access points into Galbraith Station. Added to that, after Walter's arrest, Carlisle should have felt safe enough to use one of his usual routes. The arsons had been "solved" and the manpower Murdoch had thrown into the case was supposedly reduced.

"Are there any rod holders welded on the back?" asked Carter.

O'Halloran swore beneath his breath. "None."

"Then that's our boy. Radio Murdoch, tell him our plans just changed; he's already here."

Carter retrieved the Glock he kept in his bedside table. The handgun was light and reliable—a standard-issue police weapon—which meant the gun and the ammunition were relatively easy to obtain. He checked the load on the clip, slotted the magazine in place then slipped the gun in the waistband at the small of his back.

Pulling on a black knit cap to hide his light hair, he exited the house through the French doors that faced the beach. The line of Dani's house was a solid silhouette against the night sky. Her light was out which meant she had finally gone to bed.

He checked the kitchen door and a window. Satisfied that she was safe, he ghosted along the edge of the trees, heading for the barn and outbuildings. He knew she had locked up, because he had watched her do it.

Chapter 16

Moonlight slid through a narrow gap where the drapes weren't quite pulled to, gleaming off polished wood floorboards and an elegant Edwardian dresser set against the wall. Cold light reflected off the mirror, making a ghostly image on the wall.

Punching her pillow into shape again, Dani turned over. The mattress was new, but the bed was old and in need of repair. The faint creak of the wire-woven base was almost indiscernible, but tonight every sound registered. The bed was also an antique, carved from the same oak as the dresser and the escritoire in the corner. All part of the set of furniture one of the Galbraith brides had received as a wedding gift from her husband.

Weddings. Dani stared at the intricate plaster

moulding in the centre of the ceiling. That was the trouble. In this house she had always been surrounded by wedding memorabilia. Almost every piece of furniture had had a romantic or funny story passed down with it—all connected with the comfortable, seemingly inevitable continuation of the Galbraith family line.

Now that most of the furniture was gone, and with it the stories, the house felt hollow and empty, as if its heart had been taken away. The Galbraith bad luck had finally peaked.

With a restless movement, she shifted sideways on the bed, trying to find a cool spot. Despite the air fanning down from the ceiling, the temperature seemed to be rising.

The muffled roar of the waves had grown louder, and with it the sound of the wind in the trees. Stifling a yawn, Dani leaned over and switched on her bedside lamp.

The darkness remained absolute.

Either the bulb had blown or the power was out.

Frowning, she pushed to her feet, felt her way across the room and opened the drapes. Fantasies of grey sheets of subtropical rain pounding on the roof and dripping from trees died as she stared at the sky. A waning moon hung over the water, surrounded by ragged cloud, but the trees were barely moving and the wind was minimal.

She shoved damp hair back from her face. The air was warm and close—even the floorboards felt hot.

That was because they *were* hot.

Dani stared at the floor where pale moonlight angled across the bare boards. A wisp of smoke drifted between her feet. She had been wrong. The Galbraith bad luck hadn't peaked, it was still on the rise.

The faint roaring wasn't the surf, or the wind.

Someone had set a fire beneath the house.

The flames were growing, even though the progress of the fire seemed painfully slow, impeded as it was by the lack of wind, and only visible if you crawled under the house, but even so the satisfaction Carlisle thought he would feel was eaten away by something else.

Slipping into the stygian cavern of the barn, he shrugged out of his knapsack and set it on the floor. His chest and belly felt tight; the tension that gripped him was close to suffocating. The night wasn't proceeding as he'd planned. Something was wrong.

His gaze was drawn upward. A small red dot winked in the corner. For a moment he thought he was staring at a firefly, although he had never seen one outside of a cave, and this was bright, the colour too red.

He stepped closer to the light—risked turning on his flashlight—and found himself staring directly into the lens of a camera.

Dani tried the main light switch in the bedroom. The power was definitely out. The blackout took on a more sinister connotation. Either the fire had burned through wiring, or whoever had set it had tampered with the electrics. There was a faint possibility that this wasn't arson, that the electrics themselves had failed and started the fire, but Dani didn't think so. Everything else about the house might be antique, but the wiring was modern. Robert Galbraith had had the house rewired the year before he'd died.

Pulling open a drawer, she grabbed jeans, socks and a shirt and quickly dressed. As she made her way down the hallway and took a left into the mudroom, she thumbed the emergency number into her cell phone.

A drift of smoke clogged her nostrils and stung her eyes as Dani began relaying details. Feeling along the shelf next to the door, she found the flashlight that was kept there and flicked it on. The smoke was thicker here than in the rest of the house, pouring up through floorboards that were rougher and set further apart, courtesy of a conversion that had enclosed what used to be part of the porch, turning it into a utility room.

The operator paused and queried her name.

With jerky movements Dani juggled the phone while pulling on boots. If this had been a movie she would have seen the humour in the situation, but with her throat already raw, her lungs burning, it was hard to smile at the fact that while she had never spoken to this particular operator, he had heard of her. "Yeah it's me. Again."

She reached for the key, which usually lived in the

lock. Frowning when she didn't find it, she tried the handle. The door wouldn't budge. Grimly, she yanked at the handle again. It was locked and the key was missing. Skin crawling, because if she hadn't removed the key from the door that meant someone else had, she backed out of the mudroom and slammed the door closed on the smoke. The key had definitely been there when she'd checked all the doors and windows before bed. For it to be missing now meant that whoever had stolen it had come inside the house to get it while she was lying in bed—and to do that they would have already had to have a key.

The implications piled up. To already have a key meant the person had stolen one earlier, had it copied, then replaced it. That added up to three visits.

Coughing, eyes stinging, she terminated the call, slipped the phone into her jeans pocket and made her way into the kitchen.

The keyboard, which hung on the wall next to the back door, was empty. Every key had been removed.

Cold grew in her stomach as she tried first the kitchen door, then a set of French doors off the lounge. Both were locked. Logic told Dani there was no use trying any of the other doors: as they had been at Dora's house, they would all be locked. The sabotage wasn't enough to imprison, but it had already confused and delayed her, giving the fire more time to take hold.

Holding her shirt clamped over her nose and

mouth, Dani unlatched one of the sash windows in the lounge and pushed upward.

Gulping in fresh air, she gripped the sill, flashlight in one hand, and climbed out, half stumbling, half falling into the herbaceous border. Pushing to her feet, Dani unhooked the clinging tendrils of a rose and played the beam of the flashlight over the side of the house. Thick smoke billowed from beneath it.

Chest tight, she found the hose where it was always kept, neatly coiled at the base of the main water supply—a six-thousand-gallon tank that fed the house. As she flicked on the tap, her boots sank into mud. Her jaw tightened as she tested the water pressure. Everywhere else in Jackson's Ridge the ground was as hard as iron: for the mud to be that soft, it meant a lot of water had soaked into the ground recently. It was possible the tap or the hose had a leak, but she didn't think so. She wasn't slapdash with repairs and lately she'd been keeping a close eye on all the water systems. If the hose had developed a leak, she would have known about it.

Grimly, she hauled hose around the side of the house, laying it out as she went. The light from her flashlight picked up details she'd missed before; scattered chunks of wood on the ground, and a dark hole where the hatch to the underside of the house had been left open. Crouching down, Dani directed the flashlight into the smoke-filled cavity. The beam of light was swallowed up within a few feet, but she didn't need the flashlight to see the orange glow that lit the far corner of the house.

The house itself was raised on piles with a deep timber skirt. As a kid she'd crawled under every draughty inch of it. In places the crawl space had been large enough for her to stand up in, in others she'd had to crawl on her belly.

Whoever had set the fire had known what he was doing. He'd used her own wood supply to start it, had set the fire at the point where the house was set low to the ground, then left the hatch open to help fan the flames. With the rising sea breeze, the hollow area was acting like a wind tunnel, sucking flames along the structural timbers.

Working feverishly, Dani pulled the hose further along, found a gap in the timber skirting and began to spray the flames with water. Steam billowed along with smoke, making it difficult to assess how effective the water was. If she crawled under the house with the hose she would be able to direct the water with more accuracy, the only problem was that with the dense smoke and heat she would be overcome within minutes. Her dilemma died an abrupt death when the stream of water dropped to a trickle, then stopped altogether.

Dani stared at the dripping end of the hose. Yesterday, she had had less than a quarter of a tank, which equated to over one thousand gallons of water—enough to run the hose for a good hour. If the tank was empty now, there was only one reason—someone had drained it.

Dragging the hose with her, she backed away from the heat and smoke. Her foot caught on something lying on the ground, and the beam of her flashlight picked out a familiar shape. Bending, she retrieved the axe, which was protruding from beneath one of the leggy hydrangeas that grew rampant in this part of the garden. A chill went down her spine. She hadn't moved the axe from its usual place, propped up beside the woodpile, just as she hadn't removed all the keys and locked the doors.

Someone had been prowling around her place for weeks now, familiarising themselves with the house and outbuildings and finding out where everything was kept.

She'd dismissed her uneasiness and the feeling that she was somehow connected with the arsonist as the product of coincidence and an over-active imagination, but she wasn't imagining this. Someone had drained her water tank, locked her in her own house and set it on fire while she supposedly slept, then removed any tools that could possibly be used to rescue her.

The malice and premeditation were chilling. If she hadn't been too restless to sleep, in all probability she would never have woken up.

When Dora's house had burned down, the locked doors had seemed a nasty and potentially lethal twist aimed at a disabled pensioner. Now Dani was abruptly certain that she had been the target all along.

A thud followed by a splintering sound jerked her head up. Flicking the flashlight off, Dani backed into the cover of a tall, weeping rhododendron, her fingers closing around the handle of the axe. Seconds later a dark figure flowed over the sill of the same window she'd used to exit the house.

The man straightened in the deep pool of shadow cast by the house. His head swivelled, gaze locking with hers, as if she were plainly visible. When she'd grabbed clothing she hadn't cared about the colour; she had pulled on the first things she'd found. Coincidentally, her clothes were all dark; she should have been invisible.

Reaching up, he tugged at his head. Relief shuddered through her when she caught the gleam of blond hair. Carter.

"I thought I was going to be too late." Stepping toward her, he tossed the scrap of black—a woollen cap—to the ground and jerked her into his arms, his grip momentarily crushing.

"You're supposed to be in Auckland."

"I had a change of plan."

"You mean you never left," she said with sudden insight. Carter and Murdoch had been cooking up schemes for days.

Dani leaned into his warmth, breathing in Carter's familiar, comforting scent. "The fire engine's on the way." The cold in the pit of her stomach intensified as he loosened his hold and stepped away. "All the doors were locked."

"Until about thirty seconds ago. You're going to need a new kitchen door."

The breeze gusted. Dani stared at the house and the smoke billowing from beneath it. The building was over one hundred years old and built of tinder-dry kauri, by the time the fire engine got here there wouldn't be anything left. "In a few minutes there won't *be* a house. The main tank's dry."

A short burst of static distracted Carter, and for the first time she noticed the lip mike. Her chill deepened as he relayed the information that she was all right. If she'd needed an answer as to why Carter was out this late, dressed in black, she had it.

"Murdoch and his men are searching the grounds, but it looks like our boy has given us the slip."

Carter directed the flashlight beam into the shrubs surrounding the house. "What about your back-up tank?"

Dani directed her own flashlight at a lichen-encrusted tank almost completely enshrouded by honeysuckle. The tank was old, and it leaked. It was kept functioning as an emergency supply for when the main tank was exhausted. "There's a problem. It feeds directly into the house; it doesn't have a hose connection."

And the other hose wasn't connected to the main plumbing system—it came straight out of the tank— one of the vagaries of a water system that had been constructed before either of them had been born.

Carter examined the tank. He knew the practicalities of the situation as well as she did. They could connect the house hose up with Dani's garden supply—a small corrugated iron tank that caught the water off the barn roof—but they still wouldn't have enough hose to reach the house. They could try getting more hose from Carter's place, but even if he had enough, by the time they got organized it would be too little, too late.

Carter knocked on the tank—midway the sound was flat and solid, indicating the tank was close to half full. Ironically, they had their water supply, and it was only metres from the centre of the blaze—but for all the use the water was, it could have been a mile away.

Carter took the axe from her fingers.

"What are you doing?"

"Thinking outside the square."

With a fluid movement he chopped at the base of the tank. Comprehension dawned. The house was built on a slope, tilting toward the ocean. The slope wasn't much, but it was enough. Lately, things had gotten certifiably creepy on Galbraith, but the last she'd heard, water still flowed downhill.

The night took on a surreal quality as Carter adjusted his grip on the axe and swung again. A repetitive buzzing sound caught her attention. Her phone.

Thumbing a button, she answered the call. The familiar voice of the emergency services operator registered. "Hang on a minute," Dani said, stepping further away from the water tank. As she did so, she absently noticed that the back of her hand was covered in a gleaming tracery of blood. One of the rose thorns must have sliced into her skin; she hadn't felt a thing.

The wire-reinforced concrete of the tank chipped and buckled, water spurted. Carter continued to swing, using short chopping motions, marking out a broad circle of damage. When the circle was complete, he sent the head of the axe crashing through the centre. The entire section exploded outward, water gushed from the gaping hole, soaking Carter and sweeping beneath the house in a torrent.

Chapter 17

The fire under the house reduced to smouldering damp timbers, the E.T.A. of the fire engines just minutes away, Carter did a quick tour of the house then reappeared in the kitchen.

"Where's the furniture?"

Dani blinked. In the adrenaline rush of dealing with the fires, she'd forgotten that she'd virtually emptied the house—and Carter's likely reaction. "It had to be sold."

Carter said something short and succinct. "Who to?"

Dani gave him the name of the used-furniture dealer.

"You should have told me. I would have helped."

Dani's jaw tensed. "I don't need charity."

For a long moment Carter was utterly still, his face expressionless. "It wouldn't have been charity."

Too late, Dani realized she had offended Carter on a level that had nothing to do with controlling either her or their relationship. She had instinctively always fought against Carter's macho, take-charge attitude, but that was like fighting the testosterone that made him male. With the women in his life, Carter would always react in the same way. He was male, therefore he was in charge and would provide.

A hiss of static broke the silence. Carter spoke into his lip mike, his voice terse. When he was finished he turned on his heel. He paused at the kitchen door. "Stay here where I can see you through the window. O'Halloran's just spotted something over by the barn. I'll be back in a minute." Then he strode out of the kitchen and melted into the night.

Dani let out a breath. He wasn't about to push the issue now. He'd checked every room of the house, but he still had to check the outbuildings.

Knowing Carter, he wouldn't bother with any further discussion with the furniture; he would ring the dealer direct and coldly demand the furniture was returned. She wouldn't want to be in Docherty's shoes if he had sold any of it.

Placing her flashlight on the kitchen counter, Dani reached into a cupboard and found the medical kit. As she lifted the plastic container off the shelf, the back of her hand brushed against cool metal—a fire extinguisher. Blinking, she stared at an object that was so familiar she had forgotten it was there, placed near the stove for kitchen emergencies.

A breeze sifted through the windows over the sink, making the filmy curtains shiver as she set the medical kit down on the kitchen counter. Despite the familiarity of the room, with the added distortion of the beam from the flashlight, the shifting shadows took on an eerie aspect.

A small shudder moved down Dani's spine—a touch of déjà vu—as she unfastened the plastic lid and began rummaging through the contents until she found sticking plaster and a tube of antiseptic.

"Get real," she muttered to herself. Whoever the arsonist was, he was a coward—but a clever one—which was why he hadn't been caught. He set his fires and ran, but she couldn't shift a feeling of apprehension. Coward or not, he was dangerous.

Paper rustled, preternaturally loud in the dim quiet of the kitchen, as she unwrapped a plaster and laid it ready to use. The plastic cap of the tube of lotion clicked on the bench, the smell of antiseptic lotion filled her nostrils—and something else.

Dani's head came up, all the small hairs at her nape lifting as she turned and stared in the direction of the living room. She could smell gasoline.

Something moved at the edge of her vision and a chill raced down her spine. With slow, careful movements, she reached upward. Her fingers brushed against the cool cylindrical shape of the fire extinguisher and closed over the plastic handle. "Carter?"

Movement flickered again. A whooshing sound, followed by a flickering glow sent a sickening jolt of adrenaline through her veins. A split second later a shadowy figure, backlit by flames, stepped into the kitchen.

Jaw set, pulse racing, she lifted the extinguisher off its hook. It wasn't a full-sized extinguisher, but it was heavy.

Eyes glittered in a blacked-out face as he charged, and time seemed to slow and freeze as she aimed the extinguisher and depressed the lever. A heartbeat shuddered past. Nothing happened.

She'd forgotten there was a safety feature—a tiny piece of plastic that had to be removed before the lever could be depressed.

In a convulsive movement, she threw the cylinder and ducked to one side. The extinguisher hit him full in the chest, slowing his momentum, but, as he reeled off balance, his shoulder caught hers, bouncing Dani back against the kitchen counter. Hard fingers sank into her arm and panic exploded. He was close enough that she could feel the heat from his body, smell the sharp scent of sweat. Acting purely on instinct, Dani grabbed the flashlight, which was placed on the counter and brought it smashing down on his head.

With a guttural snarl, he released his hold and clutched at the side of his face.

Fingers numbed, but still locked in a death grip on the flashlight, Dani lunged for the door. Halfway across the room a hand caught at the fabric of her shirt. Jerking free, she threw the flashlight. The glare of the beam flashed over his blacked-out face, already lit by the glow of the fire—a macabre freeze frame as he ducked and kept coming. In desperation, Dani put the width of the kitchen table between them and grasped at the only other object in reach, a broom propped against the wall, but before she could swing it, a dark form rocketed past her. Carter.

The two men caromed against the far wall, then reeled back, a blur of movement as they smashed into the table, sending it sliding into the wall. The thud of flesh on flesh was followed by a grunt and the hiss of laboured breathing. A chair was overturned, another splintered as both men went down. A split second later, Carter rolled to his feet and the two men engaged again.

Pulse pounding, and keeping clear of the brawling men, Dani inched around the kitchen until her fingers closed on the fire extinguisher. She didn't know if it would work—it had been stored in the same cupboard for years—but she had to try.

Picking up the flashlight on the way, she raced into the lounge. Smoke and heat filled the room. Several fires had been set and flames had already consumed the drapes on all of the windows and were licking at faded and peeling wallpaper. The old horsehair sofa—the only antique Docherty had refused to take, and the only remaining piece of furniture in the room—smouldered against one wall, refusing to burn. If it had been made of modern materials by now the room would have been an inferno.

Eyes stinging, lungs burning, Dani dropped the flashlight, wrenched the plastic safety guard off the extinguisher and depressed the lever. Her fear that the device wouldn't work dissolved as powdery white chemical blasted the nearest fire, instantly extinguishing the flames and coating the charred wall in a thick residue. Systematically, she worked her way around the room, putting out the fires, aware that the chemical wouldn't last more than a few seconds, leaving the sofa until last. When the canister was exhausted, she backed, choking and coughing from the room. Emptied of most of its furniture, smoke-blackened and charred, it bore little resemblance to the elegant reception room it once had been.

Blue and red lights flickered through the hallway. Blankly, Dani registered the wail of a siren. The fire engine had finally arrived. And so had Murdoch.

Dropping the extinguisher, she picked up the flashlight and stepped into the kitchen. At first glance the room was filled with uniformed police and firemen. Someone had lit a lamp, and the soft glow revealed the extent of the damage. Chairs were smashed beyond repair—the table had a crack clear down its centre. Shards of crockery and the contents of the first aid kit littered the floor, and the pantry door was hanging off its hinges, displaying the fact that several shelves had collapsed.

A dark form was lying unmoving on the floor. Carter stepped through the chaos, lifted the man's head and jerked off the balaclava.

His face was battered, one eye already swelling, but his features were easily recognisable.

George Lynch.

She had known Lynch for years, ever since he'd bought a seaside cottage, but she'd never paid him much attention. Now she registered the scar under one eye, the faint bend to his nose where it had been broken. For a split second time wavered, the sense of déjà vu disorienting, the old fear, visceral and fresh.

She remembered the wreckage of his face twenty-two years ago after *she* had hit him, the flat glitter of his gaze. Then, he had barely registered her existence, but she remembered him. "George Lynch."

Carter caught her hand and pulled her close. "Real name, Jordan Carlisle."

Dani leaned into Carter's strength. Her father. The one piece of information she had always resisted knowing, that Susan had never wanted to discuss because she had been protecting Dani.

Lynch/Carlisle's eyes flickered, caught on hers and settled into a cold stare, and suddenly she knew what else he'd done.

"*You* were driving the truck."

After years of trying, he had finally succeeded; he had killed Susan.

Chapter 18

Murdoch crouched down and checked Carlisle's condition. "A one-man crime wave. Isn't that right, Carlisle?"

Dani's stomach twisted as a flood of old memories renewed themselves. "*He was driving the truck.*"

Murdoch's gaze connected with hers, and she saw the moment he registered exactly what Lynch/Carlisle had done.

Sadness and the remnants of grief shivered through her. She had held herself responsible for the accident, but there was no way she could have avoided Carlisle; he had been aiming for the car.

Carter didn't have to ask what Dani meant. With Dani there was only one truck—the six-wheeler that had driven her off the road and killed Susan and

Robert. He hadn't checked that report and he could kick himself; it was the one connection he hadn't made, and the most vital. Carlisle/Lynch had outsmarted them all. He'd been lying low in Jackson's Ridge for years under an assumed identity. In that time he'd managed to successfully murder Susan and Robert; then he'd waited until Dani was alone and isolated, with Ellen dead and David away at university, before he had targeted her. The only flaw in his planning was that Carter had come back.

O'Halloran stared at Carlisle. "Carlisle and Sons, the top-end legal firm in Auckland. I thought he was familiar."

Murdoch's expression turned grim. "He's the eldest son. In theory their finest and brightest. The psychiatric report doesn't make good bedtime reading."

Briefly, Murdoch filled Dani in on Carlisle's past and the part Susan had played in putting him away. She stared at Carlisle's greying hair, his unshaven jaw, the mystery of the past finally solved. According to her birth certificate, he was her father but, apart from utter revulsion at what he'd done, she felt nothing for him.

An intense sadness for the loss of her mother filled her. It was Susan who had brought her up, Susan who had taken on the mantle of parenthood. Carlisle might have fathered her biologically, but that was all he'd done. As a child the fear he'd inspired had dominated her life, he'd seemed larger than life, but not any more.

Coldly, Murdoch stepped forward and cuffed

him. One of the Mason cops began reading Carlisle his rights.

Carlisle stared at Dani, dark eyes like pebbles. "I knew you were at the wheel of that car."

Carter's expression grew cold enough to send a chill down Dani's spine.

He caught Carlisle's gaze and held it and Carlisle seemed to shrink in on himself. "First-degree murder," Carter said softly, "on two counts, with two further charges of attempted murder and arson. Even if the jail terms run concurrently they'll be impressive. If you only serve twenty years, by the time you get out you'll be an old man. And if you do get out, *I'll* know about it."

Murdoch hauled Carlisle to his feet. "And if you're thinking of applying for parole early, don't. The psychiatric report's going to rewrite the text books."

Carlisle's face went a dull red. A split second later he exploded, but surrounded by cops, he didn't stand a chance. Abruptly Carlisle's expression smoothed out and became frighteningly normal. "Susan's death was an accident. The court made a ruling."

Murdoch jerked his head at one of the Mason cops, indicating he wanted Carlisle moved out. "You're forgetting the fundamentals. Just because the case was closed, doesn't mean it can't be reopened if new evidence comes to light."

O'Halloran stiffened. "I can smell smoke."

Carlisle's mouth twisted into a grimace. "You haven't found that one yet."

O'Halloran felt his stomach turn. He stared at Carlisle and abruptly something inside of him clicked back into its right perspective. The man who had torched his house and killed his wife and child had been like this. He had seen his face; seen his eyes and, like Carlisle, nothing about him had added up. For over a year he had wondered what he could have done to avert the tragedy and save his family. The answer was depressing, but it finally made sense. Nothing.

He had no better chance than Rawlings of predicting when a mentally unstable criminal decided they would do harm, let alone why.

Flames flared as a container of diesel caught alight, sending heat rolling out into the night and momentarily illuminating the faces of the fire crew as they fought to bring the fire under control. Dani stepped back as Jim McCarthy, who had taken over as fire chief now that Walter had been removed from the roll, strode around the perimeter of the fire and roared at one of his men.

The ignition point had been in the tractor shed, but the flames threatened to jump the small alleyway between the shed and the barn and set the barn alight. The angle of the hose was adjusted, sending the water in lower. Seconds later a cloud of steam erupted from the centre of the flames and the fire was out.

Shivering in the cool night air, Dani studied the smoking skeleton of the shed, the twisted wreckage of the tractor and the scorched side of the barn. With the old Ferguson gone, it felt like the end of an era. As problematic as the Dinosaur had been, it had been a link to the past—a seemingly solid, immutable part of Galbraith—and she would miss it.

Change was in the air. She could feel it in the turn of the season, the bite of ozone in the air. Summer was over, and she was no longer needed at Galbraith. Aside from the two horses, there was no livestock to care for. The house was empty and blank, a clean slate, waiting for David to move in and eventually repair the damage and turn it into a home.

She'd stubbornly resisted thinking about stepping into a new life, but now the moment was here, she didn't know if she was ready.

Murdoch studied Lynch as Lowell put him in the back of the cruiser. Even though he'd known for the last twenty-four hours who the likely perpetrator was, he still had trouble crediting that George Lynch was Jordan Carlisle. In all his years on the force, the baffling series of arsons had been the most frustrating case he'd ever worked—not least because he was dealing with people he had known—or thought he had known—for years.

If Carter hadn't asked him to check into Susan Marlow's past, the investigation would still be dragging on.

As a criminal Carlisle was a surprising package, and Murdoch wasn't often surprised. Using Walter's arson as a cover for his own crimes had been nothing short of genius. But, criminal flair aside, Carlisle's downfall had always been pre-ordained. His obsessive need for revenge had ultimately aided in his capture, and further down the line would give Murdoch all the motivational evidence he needed to secure a conviction.

Murdoch flipped open the boot of the cruiser and took custody of the evidence: a knapsack containing lighters and an empty container of a popular firelighting gel that was used for outdoor fire pots. His expression was grim as he filled out the paperwork and signed it off. There was no way he was losing chain of custody on this evidence. Carlisle's capture had successfully closed eighty percent of Jackson's Ridge's unsolved crimes—including one that had never been suspected.

The Mason cops put Lynch in the back seat of the cruiser. Lowell slammed the door closed and walked around to the front passenger seat.

Murdoch frowned. "Lowell, get in the back with Carlisle." There was no way he was driving the vehicle with Lynch unattended in the back.

Lowell glanced at O'Halloran.

Murdoch didn't bother to hide his impatience. "Last week you were drinking in the pub with him— *and* he's cuffed."

O'Halloran took the front seat. "Don't worry, he doesn't have a weapon."

They'd made sure of that. Lynch had deceived a lot of people, but unless he'd devised a way to store a weapon internally he was clean. In any case the ball was in Murdoch's court on that one. O'Halloran was on official, but unpaid, leave, but even if he was being paid, he wasn't highly motivated to pull on a pair of rubber gloves.

Murdoch glanced at Carter as he slid behind the wheel. "By the way, this afternoon someone reported a couple of ostriches out on the point. If my memory serves me rightly, that land belongs to you."

One of the cold-eyed cops from Mason actually cracked a grin. "Could be a breeding pair."

Carter closed Murdoch's door. "You guys are funny. Real funny."

The two cops from Mason left in a cloud of dust. O'Halloran lifted a hand as Murdoch turned the key in the ignition. "See you around, Rawlings."

"Count on it." Carter watched until Murdoch's vehicle disappeared around the bend.

If there was one guy he wanted to see off the premises, cop or not, it was O'Halloran. He'd said he wasn't interested in Dani, but Carter wouldn't believe that until O'Halloran found himself a woman. And he would know when that happened, because he was going to keep tabs on him. O'Halloran was due back at Auckland Central in a week's time. It just so happened that Carter had contacts there. He was also owed a favour, and he would be calling it in. O'Halloran wouldn't be able to go to the bathroom without Carter finding out about it.

Carter found Dani watching the fire crew roll up the hose. Linking his fingers with hers, he pulled her into his arms, wrapping her in close. She looked pale and shaken, and she felt as fragile as a bird. His jaw tightened. Worn down from years of guilt and fear, and months of running Galbraith Station on her own.

He had always gone where he felt he could make a difference. For years Jackson's Ridge had never been that destination, but all the time it had been riddled with crime and intrigue—a time bomb waiting to explode.

It wasn't often he missed not just a few clues, but all of them. His neighbours had been murdered and Carlisle had been living right under their noses, a rundown cottage and an apparent lack of money the prime props for the double life he'd been leading. A convicted felon, Carlisle had played a cat and mouse game—not only physically, but financially—with all the locals, exacting his revenge on the community that had made Susan and Dani welcome.

As the fire crew left, Dani pushed free and started toward the house. Carter caught her hand. "Leave it. You're moving in with me."

She looked bemused. "I should have something to say about that."

"Say it in the morning."

Dani wasn't about to argue. She was dirty, tired, and she was mortally sick of fires.

The short walk across the paddock that separated the two houses passed in a daze. Dani blinked as they stepped up onto the veranda and Carter pulled her straight into his bedroom. She lifted a brow. "Romantic."

The beginnings of a smile twitched at his mouth. "You know me."

For the first time that night warmth broke through the ice that had encased her ever since Carlisle had started his attack.

Relinquishing his grip he walked to a chest of drawers, slipped something in his pocket, grabbed her hand and pulled her out the door.

"The beach?"

"Humour me." This time he was going to do it right. No more half measures.

Tiredness slid away to be replaced by an entirely new tension as she let Carter pull her down the shell path that wound downhill. The beach had always been neutral ground—more or less—although some days it was so crowded with memories there was no peace there.

The moon slid out from behind a heavy bank of cloud and Dani's heart rate increased, it was fear pure and simple. She had an idea what it was that Carter had slipped in his pocket.

Carter pulled her to within a few metres of the sea. The tide was in, the swell almost nonexistent, the water glassy.

A morepork hooted in the distance, the cry lonely enough to make the back of her throat ache as he took both of her hands in his.

"Danielle Margaret Marlow, will you marry me?"

The words were clear and distinct, with no room for ambiguity. The use of her full name added an old-fashioned formality that made her stomach tighten.

She stared at their linked fingers. "When did you decide?"

"About six years ago."

She swallowed. He was serious.

"I got the ring out of the bank when I came back last time."

But he hadn't asked her because she'd already started to close him out. She'd turned down his suggestion that they live together, then he'd been airlifted out to Indonesia and she had almost lost him permanently.

Her fingers tightened. "I don't want to lose you again." The words were straightforward, but the baggage that went with them wasn't. She wanted with an extremity that hurt.

"You won't, whether you agree to marry me or not, but I'd like our kids to have my name."

Arrested, she stared at him. Carter and children. The thought made her dizzy.

They had never talked about permanence and kids. She'd always thought it was because Carter didn't want them, now she was beginning to see why the discussion had never taken place. Like a crab hiding in its shell, she'd been too good at protecting herself, too good at hiding her feelings.

She took a deep breath. Moonlight and the sea, and a proposal. She stared at the planes of Carter's face. She felt touched to her core—swept away. "It's hard to take in." Her heart was pounding so hard, she was having difficulty breathing.

"Take as long as you like, I'm not going anywhere. I've resigned. I wanted to give you the papers, but they haven't arrived yet. You won't be an army wife, you'll be marrying a farmer."

She took a deep breath and leaped. "Yes."

For a moment he was utterly still and she wondered if he'd heard her, then he reached into his pocket and brought out a small leather box.

Her mouth went dry. She'd seen the box with its faded gold trim and distinctive jeweller's mark sitting on his dresser shortly after he'd returned from overseas last time.

He opened the lid. Light glimmered on an antique ring with a large diamond at the centre of a cluster of smaller gemstones. Her heart squeezed tight. She recognized the ring, it was the same one worn by his great-great-grandmother in the oil painting in his hallway—a ring that had been worn by every subsequent Rawlings bride of the eldest male child since.

With slow, deliberate movements, he picked up her left hand and slid the ring on the third finger.

In the moonlight the stones gleamed softly. The ring fitted as if it had been made for her. She touched the central diamond with a fingertip, and a warm shiver went through her. It was crazy, but in that moment she felt the whisper of generation upon generation of love and devotion.

A droplet landed on her cheek, then another.

Carter touched his lips to hers. When he lifted his head the moon was blotted out by cloud.

Dazed, Dani registered that the drought had broken; it was raining. Wrapping her arms around his neck, she kissed him back, sinking into Carter's bedrock warmth and strength. Finally, after years of travelling, she'd come home.

Chapter 19

The day before the wedding, Dani and Becca arrived for a final fitting at Harriet's town house in Mason.

It had been two months since Carter had proposed and almost that long since the mortgage payment had been met and David had moved back into the Galbraith house. With the bank's new refinancing options, David had been able to repair the house, restock the farm and buy a new tractor. He was still stretched financially, and he would be for a while, but Galbraith was finally on an even keel.

Once the drought-breaking rain had started it hadn't stopped. Any fear of another copycat arsonist had been washed away in a deluge of water and bright green growth. They were on the edge of winter, but spring was definitely in the air. Relieved farmers were grinning, kids were happily splashing about in muddy gumboots, and mothers and wives were groaning at the extra laundry. The syndicate that had been buying up properties had folded, causing a minor ripple in the stock market. Carlisle's brokering firm had crashed, and Bainbridge had been removed from the board of directors, his financial activities now under the scrutiny of a special commission for high-level fraud.

At last report, Carlisle was being held on remand without bail, pending trial, and Bainbridge had left the country, tailed by Flynn, who had tracked him to the Caribbean, where he was holed up in an exclusive island resort with a "close friend." Flynn had sold the story to a national daily with a follow-up exposé to a prominent glossy magazine. The massive injection of capital had saved Flynn from imminent bankruptcy, and the *Chronicle* from oblivion.

Wells, armed with an embarrassing arsenal of facts about Bainbridge meddling with the bank, had exerted pressure on the directors and freed up a number of mortgages, including Tom Stoddard's and the Galbraiths'. The bank hadn't changed its motto, but it was finally starting to live up to it.

Harriet opened the front door and promptly ushered Dani and Becca upstairs to one of the spare rooms, where a designer box lay in state on the bed.

Once she'd agreed to the wedding, Aunt Harriet and Becca had started making arrangements and pulling strings. Harriet had contacts that extended beyond the jewellery business into the world of haute couture. Under Harriet's strict eye, a design was agreed upon and commissioned—and she had insisted on paying for the dress as a wedding gift.

When the white silk gown was shaken out of folds of tissue paper, Dani let out a breath. It was going to be all right.

Minutes later, she stared at her reflection, dazed. The bodice was a sleeveless shell that left her shoulders and arms bare. It fell in a long, elegant line to her feet. Becca fitted the veil and stood back.

For long moments, Dani stared at her reflection in Harriet's full-length mirror. Her hair was in a plait, she wasn't wearing any makeup, but none of that mattered—the dress made her beautiful.

Harriet stared critically at the effect. "We're going to have to cut your hair."

Becca nodded. "And do something with those nails."

"I'm not shortening my hair."

"The length is fine, dear," Harriet said smoothly. "I'll just get Jose to trim the ends and take a little weight out."

"Jose?"

Harriet lifted the curtain and peered out at the front driveway. "He cuts for the best salon in Mason. I think he's just arrived."

Minutes later, back in her own clothes, Dani found herself seated in Harriet's sunny front parlour with Jose—a tall, faintly Asian-looking man—fussing over her hair.

Dani stared at the hairdressing and manicurist's paraphernalia. Between the foil wrap and coveralls, hi-tech headgear and machinery, there was enough equipment to outfit a mission to Mars. Someone should tell NASA. "Do I have to have the nails?"

Becca lifted a brow. "How many times are you planning on getting married?"

Just one.

Dani sat down and gave herself over. "Point taken."

The church was full; the bride was late. Carter glanced at his watch.

His best man, Gabriel West, looked relaxed. "It's traditional."

The vicar checked his watch, the organist frowned, taking Carter back to his childhood, when she'd glared at him for singing off-key. He checked his watch again.

Ten minutes later, the limousine nosed into the space reserved in front of the church. Pushing the driver's door open, Dani exited the car, not waiting for David to make his way around to open the door. After the interminable wait to have, of all things, a tire changed, she was in no mood to play ladies.

Taking care the hem of the dress didn't get smeared with dirt, Dani strode through the pretty archway that fronted the church and up the cobbled path. Carter was waiting on the steps.

She started up the steps, trying to look composed.

"You waited." And until that moment she hadn't known just how frightened she'd been that he wouldn't.

"I wasn't about to let you get away this time."

Carter's fingers closed over hers, pulling her close and a jolt of recognition went through her. His gaze was cool, his jaw set as hard as adamantine. She'd seen that look before: when he'd been fifteen and his horse had broken a leg and Carter had insisted he was the one who had to put Jerry down. Again when he'd been twenty-five and his father had had a serious heart attack and had had to leave the farm. Carter had insisted on buying his parents out, enabling them to have a comfortable stress-free retirement. She knew that expression with the intimacy, the familiarity, of years and the primitive sense of recognition shimmered through her again. She *knew* him, almost as well as she knew herself—maybe even better. A piercing sweetness moved through her and suddenly she had her moment; the confirmation she had needed.

Carter loved her; he had always loved her. If she hadn't showed, he would have come after her, and he wouldn't have stopped until he'd found her and brought her back. "The car broke down."

"I thought that was my line."

"Not any more." She crossed the fingers of one hand behind her back that this was the last hitch. She'd jumped through enough hoops, all she wanted to do was get married.

David strode up the steps, and handed Dani her bouquet. Clearing his throat, he gave Carter a stern look. "Shouldn't you be in the church?"

With a last cold glance at the limousine, Carter released her and turned on his heel. Dani had the distinct impression that he would prefer to escort her up the aisle himself—just to make sure.

The last of the tension and strain that had marred the morning melted away as Dani lifted the veil over her face, checked her bouquet and placed her hand on Tom's arm. A curious sense of calmness descended on her as they stepped into the vestibule, and the first strains of the "Wedding March" floated out into the warm afternoon air.

The wedding reception was held in the Jackson's Ridge community hall, a long low building that was almost as old as the pub and which had originally been an army barracks.

Carter glanced at the copper plaque that outlined the history of the building. "Can't seem to get away from the job."

Harriet reached inside a plastic carry bag and handed Dani a familiar case. "Here's your real wedding gift."

Dani opened the lid. Her grandmother's jewellery was still displayed exactly as she'd placed it. She was willing to bet Harriet hadn't even opened the box; she had simply kept it for her. Moisture blurred her vision. "You said you had a buyer for these."

Both Harriet's eyebrows elevated. "I lied."

David slipped a handkerchief along with an envelope into her hands. "You'd better open this before you leave."

Carefully blotting the tears, she opened the envelope. It contained a legal document. "You can't give me this."

David shrugged. "I'm not, I simply refused to accept your gift of the shares. I know you had some silly belief that Galbraith isn't your home, but I happen to think you're wrong. Galbraith would have gone under the hammer if it wasn't for you."

Dani opened her mouth to argue.

"Don't. I'm not accepting the shares."

Carter caught her gaze. She had no problem reading the miniscule signs of body language and facial expression. It was Carter's wedding and he was on his best behaviour. It was a known fact that he liked to socialize and that he was good at it—but only to a point—and right now he was at the limit of his patience.

His hand landed in the small of her back, and she found herself discreetly hustled to a side door. An elderly lady cut a swathe through the crowd, bent on waylaying him. With a deft movement, he dipped his head and kissed her, staving off the interruption.

Long seconds later he murmured in her ear. "Let's get out of here. How about a chartered flight to a Pacific Island and two weeks at a secluded beach resort with no guns, no night-vision gear, no arsonists and no ostriches?"

Dani grinned and let Carter lead her out into the night. How was she supposed to resist that?

* * * * *

INTIMATE MOMENTS™

Psychic agent Eric Vinland's mission
to recover stolen government secrets
is jeopardized when his powers
disappear. Suddenly, he doesn't
know which is worse...being hunted
by fanatical terrorists, or his
vulnerability to the only woman
he's never been able to read,
partner Dawn Moon.

STRAIGHT THROUGH THE HEART

BY LYN STONE

Silhouette Intimate Moments
#1408

**AVAILABLE MARCH 2006
AT YOUR FAVORITE RETAIL OUTLET.**

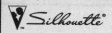

INTIMATE MOMENTS™

Reporter Darcy Sampson is
convinced a serial arsonist is still
alive and seeks out former arson
investigator Michael Gannon for
answers. When fires erupt in
Darcy's hometown, the two must
battle to solve the case and
the desires threatening to
consume them both.

THE ARSONIST

BY MARY BURTON

Silhouette Intimate Moments #1410

DON'T MISS THIS THRILLING STORY,
AVAILABLE MARCH 2006 WHEREVER
SILHOUETTE BOOKS ARE SOLD.

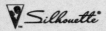
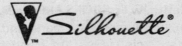

USA TODAY
BESTSELLING AUTHOR

Shirl HENKE

BRINGS YOU

SNEAK AND RESCUE
March 2006

Rescuing a brainwashed rich kid
from the Space Quest TV show
convention should have been a cinch
for retrieval specialist Sam Ballanger.
But when gun-toting thugs gave chase,
Sam found herself on the run with a truly
motley crew, including the spaced-out
teen, her flustered husband and one
very suspicious Elvis impersonator....

SBSAR

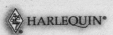

INTRIGUE

Don't miss this first title in Lori L. Harris's exciting new Harlequin Intrigue series—

THE BLADE BROTHERS OF COUGAR COUNTY

TARGETED

(Harlequin Intrigue #901)

BY LORI L. HARRIS

On sale February 2006

Alec Blade and Katie Carroll think they can start fresh in Cougar County. Each hopes to bury the unresolved events of their violent pasts. But they soon learn just how mistaken they are when a faceless menace reappears in their lives. Suddenly it isn't a matter of outrunning the past. Now they have to survive long enough to have a future.

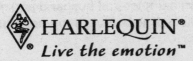

HARLEQUIN®
Live the emotion™

INTIMATE MOMENTS™

A mugging leaves attorney
Alexandra Spencer with a head
injury—and no recollection of her
recent divorce. Dylan Parker's
investigation into the not-so-random
attack is nothing compared to
the passion he feels for the woman
who once broke his heart. Can he
find answers before losing himself
to Alex—again?

MEMORIES
AFTER
MIDNIGHT

BY LINDA RANDALL WISDOM

Silhouette Intimate Moments #1409

DON'T MISS THIS THRILLING STORY,
AVAILABLE MARCH 2006 WHEREVER
SILHOUETTE BOOKS ARE SOLD.

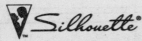

COMING NEXT MONTH

#1407 A HUSBAND'S WATCH—Karen Templeton
The Men of Mayes County
After a tornado destroys mechanic Darryl Andrew's garage,
he realizes that more than a broken arm and livelihood need
rebuilding—his marriage is in serious danger of crumbling. While
Darryl's secrets continue to plague their relationship,
Faith Meyerhauser is torn between her loyalty to her husband and
family and following a dream she's buried for nearly
twelve years.

#1408 STRAIGHT THROUGH THE HEART—Lyn Stone
Special Ops
NSA agent Dawn Moon is chosen to assist Eric Vinland, the
sexy agent whose psychic abilities are crucial in recovering stolen
government secrets. But the mission is put in jeopardy when Eric
realizes his powers have disappeared, and he doesn't know which
is worse…being hunted down by a group of terrorists, or his
vulnerability to the only woman he's never
been able to read.

**#1409 MEMORIES AFTER MIDNIGHT—
Linda Randall Wisdom**
When Alexandra Spencer is attacked in a seemingly random
mugging, a head injury causes her to forget her divorce from the
one man who can save her—police detective Dylan Parker. Dylan
senses there is more to the crime and reluctantly takes up the
investigation, but finds it hard to concentrate as he is drawn to
the kinder, gentler woman who still sparks his desires.

#1410 THE ARSONIST—Mary Burton
Reporter Darcy Sampson is convinced a serial arsonist is
still alive, and she seeks out former arson investigator
Michael Gannon for answers. When fires erupt in Darcy's
hometown, the two must battle to solve the case and the attraction
threatening to consume them both.